Farrelly's Field Guide

To

Irish Faerie Folk

FARRELLY'S FIELD GUIDE

TO

IRISH FAERIE FOLK

JOHN FARRELLY

Compiled from notes by Fantasius Farrelly

THE O'BRIEN PRESS
DUBLIN

Dedicated to the memory of Michael O'Brien – a true gentleman

First published 2024 by The O'Brien Press Ltd.
12 Terenure Road East, Rathgar, Dublin 6, D06 HD27, Ireland.
Tel: +353 1 4923333; Fax: +353 1 4922777
E-mail: books@obrien.ie; Website: obrien.ie
The O'Brien Press is a member of Publishing Ireland.

ISBN 978-1-78849-414-4

Thank you to Conor Fearon for checking the Irish spellings throughout the book.
Fantasius cottage photo (p.11) courtesy of Bernarde Kilgallon. Used with permission.
Cousin Niall photo (p.47) courtesy of Eleanor Kershaw. Used with permission.

Published in
DUBLIN
UNESCO
City of Literature

Great Irish books
O'BRIEN
obrien.ie

Up the airy mountain,
Down the rushy glen,
We daren't go a-hunting
For fear of little men.
William Allingham, *The Fairies*

The most beautiful experience we can have is the mysterious. It is the fundamental emotion which stands at the cradle of true art and true science. Whoever does not know it and can no longer wonder, no longer marvel, is as good as dead, and his eyes are dimmed.
Albert Einstein, *The World As I See It*

CONTENTS

FOREWORD

'The rarest of beasts.' That's what my uncle Kevin called me when I rocked up to help him clear out an old cottage one Sunday morning a few years ago. 'A man who turns up when he says he will.' Other strapping male members of our family were meant to be there as well, but one of them had thrown his back out by – get this – wringing out a towel. Another had achieved a sudden toothache just the night before, and a third had an appointment with a specialist he'd forgotten all about. An appointment with a specialist on a Sunday? What was he a specialist in – *duvets*?

So it was just me and my uncle Kevin. The house we were clearing out belonged to my father's, and Kevin's father's, granduncle Fantasius, which would make him my great-granduncle. The cottage had three small rooms, and had been built by some distant ancestor who had evidently taken umbrage against right angles. It stood near a prehistoric cairn in a remote area of South Armagh. So remote, in fact, that Google Earth

My great-granduncle Fantasius's cottage.

shows it as a sort of brownish-grey smudge that you could easily mistake for a clump of trees. Kevin was building a new house on the site and the cottage had to come down. And before it came down, it had to be cleared out.

I'd only met my great-granduncle Fantasius once, when my father visited him the year before he died. I was five. I don't remember much about him other than a great big, bushy beard and bright green eyes that shone over the top of it. He seemed kind and a little wild. But I do remember he took a liking to me and spent most of that afternoon teaching me the longest place name in the world, somewhere called: Taumatawhakatangihangako-auauotamateaturipukakapikimaungahoronuku-pokaiwhenuakitanatahu in New Zealand. He had been there in 1938, just before the Second World War. He broke the word down into chunks, repeating them over and over until I had it down pat. His eyes crinkled at the sides and filled with tears when I recited it for him in front of his roaring fire, his tears reflecting the orange flames. I could still say it for you to this day, almost fifty years later, if you were to buy me a couple of pints.

As Kevin and I were loading an anvil into the back of his rickety HiAce van, I asked him about Fantasius. And yes, I did say anvil. Fantasius had owned one of those things I had thus far believed to exist only in animated cartoons featuring animals trying to murder one another. Asking Kevin about my great-granduncle gave me a few moments' respite from trying to hoist it into the van. I was already aching in places I didn't know I had. Kevin, evidently glad of a break himself, plonked down on the rusty old anvil and proceeded to tell me about Fantasius.

Fantasius F Farrelly was born in 1870, the seventh of fourteen children. There were six elder boys (Fergus, Féilim, Fintan, Ferdia, Francis and Finbar) and seven younger girls (Fidelma, Fanny, Fiona, Faela, Fianna, Fionnuala and Betsy). This means he was 106 years old when he died in 1976. His father was himself from a large family and the seventh boy. This made Fantasius the seventh son of a seventh son, which apparently granted him not only healing powers, but clairvoyance as well. Fantasius also had 'Morton's Toe', which is where your second toe is longer than your big toe. This again is a sign of extra-sensory abilities, and Fantasius's were freakishly long, on both feet. This, said Kevin, enabled him to see fairies and penetrate the 'féth fíada' (magical mist) that normally shielded them from the eyes of humans.

Kevin told me all of this with a straight face. I was half-expecting him to suddenly burst out laughing, but he continued in earnest.

Once, Fantasius had traced a ley line with a dowsing rod from the cairn near his cottage straight through the local churchyard and on to a megalith several miles away. His palms were red-raw from the rod twisting around in his hands. Fantasius was well known in the area for his special gifts, and people would come to him to be healed or to sort out any problems they were having with the fairies.

Now, I don't know about you, but when someone says the word 'fairies', I immediately think of wee, tiny humans with wings, flitting about the woods, wearing sewn-together leaves and hats made from foxgloves. That and the fact they don't

exist. But Kevin assured me that Irish people just a generation or two ago had absolutely believed in fairies. These fairies, however, were about as far removed from the cutesy, benevolent, modern fairy as it was possible to get. The fairies they believed in were pretty damn scary. So scary, in fact, that they were always referred to euphemistically as the 'Good People', just in case they were listening.

By the end of the day, we had most of the stuff cleared out and loaded into the back of the van. There wasn't really anything of value, but by way of reward, Kevin handed me a soggy, foul-smelling cardboard box stuffed with papers: 'You're an artist – you'll probably like this.' Gee, thanks. He chugged away down the lane, waving out the window. As I watched the van disappear around the bend in the fading light, I began to feel that here, in a lonely place like this, with no electricity, no running water and no television, a person *could* start to believe in the kinds of fairies my ancestors had. The kinds that stare in through cracked windowpanes on starless, wintry nights, when a chill wind rattles the eaves.

I packed the musty box into the boot of my car and drove away from Fantasius's cottage. That was the last I saw of it, for Kevin had it bulldozed a few months later. The old box sat forgotten on a shelf in my garage until just last year, when I found it while looking for something else, as is always the way. In it, amid copious mouse droppings, were dozens of yellowing pages, filled with handwritten notes and pencil sketches. I was taken aback by many of the drawings, which seemed to depict what I can only describe as mythical creatures. The accompanying notes, dated between the early 1890s and the late 1960s, were all written in the same hand. I sat in my cold garage under the light of a bare bulb for several hours, trying to make sense of the words and matching them with their corresponding drawings.

What I ended up with is pretty much what you are holding in your hands now. I merely interpreted Fantasius's spidery handwriting, typed up the manuscript, put the entries in alphabetical order and added a smattering of footnotes here and there (you're welcome). Fantasius evidently intended his work for publication, but he either didn't get the opportunity or simply did not publish for fear of ridicule. This assembled work appears to be the result of Fantasius F Farrelly's many years of field research into the beguiling subject of Irish folklore, where he claims to have encountered dozens of what we might today call cryptids, or fantastical beings.

What it **actually** is, I will have to leave up to you. There are three options as far as I can see: First, it is entirely made up by my great-granduncle – a hoax perpetrated over seven decades, only to sit festering in a box in a house slated for demolition. Second, my great-granduncle was nutty as a fruitcake.

Or third, it is absolutely genuine. And that is the option that scares me the most.

There are familiar creatures here from Irish folklore, such as the banshee and the changeling, but there are others I'd never even heard of. The amadán, anyone? How about the gancanagh? The fetch? No, me neither. This book is also full of astonishing revelations. For instance, I discovered that the most quintessentially Irish of all folkloric creatures, the leprechaun, was unknown in Ireland until medieval times. I had assumed leprechauns had always been around, appearing on cereal boxes and in bad Hollywood movies since ... forever.

Judge for yourself whether what follows is genuine or the nonsensical ravings of a lunatic mind. After you've read it, maybe we can meet for a pint to talk about it. And I can recite for you, if you're lucky, the longest place name in the world. I think Fantasius would like that.

John Farrelly, Newry, Co. Down

INTRODUCTION

ON THE NATURE OF FAERIES

Imagine, if you will, a man who is well liked by his neighbours in the town where he lives. Perhaps his family have owned a shop in the community for several generations. He is generally treated by his fellow citizens with respect as befits his station. He may have a few enemies, if they can be called such – those with whom his family has had some kind of petty feud, or perhaps those who just do not care for his character, but generally he can sleep quite easily in his bed. He observes all the laws of his community, and follows the perennial rituals and customs of day-to-day life in his town.

The same man now visits another town where he is not known, where he and his family's reputations matter not a jot and where he is viewed with suspicion. His record of achievements or the content of his character are not known there. Say this man goes to this town's square, where there is a statue of the town's founder. He is hungry and sits on the plinth of the statue to eat a cheese-and-pickle sandwich. One of the town's citizens looks upon this with abject horror and runs to fetch the town constable. Presently, the man is beaten by an angry mob, is arrested and taken to the town gaol, still mystified as to the nature of his crime. From behind bars, bruised and bloody, he begs the town constable to tell him what

transgression he has committed. Does he not know, growls the constable, that out of respect to the town's founder, no one is allowed to sit on the statue's plinth?

This is the attitude a human should adopt when dealing with the faerie realm – you are a stranger in a strange land. It can be difficult for the average human to grasp that the Aos Sí, to give them their proper title, are neither good nor evil. At best, they are ambivalent towards the human race and generally want to have no dealings with them whatsoever. They are content to live in their parallel realm unmolested and, whenever their paths do cross with ours, they generally wish to carry out their business without distraction.

When a human causes harm, whether intentionally or innocuously, faerie vengeance is swift, awful and usually disproportionate to the perceived foul. To the tiny fishes that get scooped up in its maw, the tiger shark is a terrible 'evil' that wipes out their existence. To the shark, they are simply lunch. Morals do not come into it.

I am inclined to believe that faeries dwell in a realm that exists slightly out of step with our own. They have been around for much, much longer than mankind. Some say they are the fallen angels of Biblical lore, others that they are the Tuatha

Dé Danann, driven underground by the Milesians in days of old. In any case, to them we are usurpers of *their* planet.

So to expect to receive a crock of gold or three wishes if you happen to cross paths with a faery is both naïve and very dangerous. At worst, you could end up dead or trapped in the faerie realm, a place you do not wish to be for any prolonged period. At best, expect to receive nothing except the experience of the encounter itself and you will usually be all right.

Usually.

Fantasius Farrelly

PACKING LIST

Once documenting otherworldly encounters became less of a hobby and more of a vocation, I found the following items of good use to take with me on expeditions.

1. Knapsack
2. Pencils and sketch book for recording encounters.
3. Walking stick made from rowan or ash wood – this protects against faerie magic when in the woods. Forests are heavily infested with faeries.
4. Map and compass
5. Black-hafted, iron-bladed knife – faeries hate iron, and the black handle will protect from physical and magical attack. Also for pencil sharpening and whittling.
6. *Old Moore's Almanac* (for phases of the moon, etc.).
7. *Handbook for Travellers in Ireland*
8. Spyglass
9. Tent
10. An iron horseshoe, to hang above the entrance to your tent. Hung upright like the letter 'U', it will catch and store good luck and prevent faeries from entering.
11. Sleeping mat and blanket
12. Matches in tin
13. Lantern
14. Skillet
15. Towel
16. A bag of salt – faeries fear this.
17. Ball of wax, for stoppering up ears against faerie music, known to enthral the listener.
18. Magnifying glass, for examining smaller types of faery.

19. St John's wort, for protection from faerie magic.
20. A bundle of oak, ash and hawthorn twigs, bound with red thread, will protect against faeries. I hang a bundle on my knapsack.
21. Hag stone (also known as an adder stone, witch stone or holey stone) – a stone with a hole in it that has naturally occurred, usually by running water. As well as offering some protection from faerie magic, peering through a hag stone can allow the viewer to see into the faerie realm, making the invisible visible. I don't need one, as I have the gift of second sight, but you might find it useful. Best worn on a thong around the neck for ease of use.

You may have noticed that one item I do not include is a camera. Apart from it being unwieldy in the field, faeries are notoriously camera-shy and when they are snapped, often do not show up on film.

How to Use This Book

This is intended to be a *vade mecum*[1], a handbook to assist in identifying faeries and Ireland's folkloric denizens in their natural – or supernatural – habitat. The illustrations depict encounters with various creatures and each entry gives practical information that will help the reader spot it in the field and may just save their life.

Finally, the 'notes' section gives information on the category to which the creature belongs (see below), its lifespan, its known habitat, its most common location on the island of Ireland and its magical powers, if any. There is also a size-comparison graphic and occasionally an artefact of some kind I recovered during my encounters. Some entries are cross-referenced with others.

Many folklorists use the more modern word 'fairy' and 'fairies', but I am not one of them. I prefer the more archaic terms 'faery' and 'faeries'.

William Butler Yeats gives two categories of faery: Firstly, sociable or trooping faeries, which include sheoques (land faeries) and water faeries. The second category is solitary faeries. I have expanded upon these categories – faeries tend to be in the main humanoid in appearance, and I have encountered many other creatures, some of which cannot be considered faeries as such, but are either rare beasts, such as the dobhar-chú, or faery beasts, such as the alp-luachra. Others, such as the fear liath and cailleach, are more like deities. Still others, such as the fetch, are phantasms from the spirit realm – either what the Irish call a 'thivish' (from the Gaelic word 'taibhse' meaning 'ghost') or 'undead', revenants from the Otherworld, like the sluagh na marbh.

By their very nature, faeries often defy categorisation, so I have often defaulted to the most common aggregation when trying to define these elusive creatures.

---

1 Latin for 'go with me', a *vade mecum* is a manual or guidebook compact enough to be carried in a deep pocket.

ALP-LUACHRA

'FEROCIOUS LITTLE CREATURE'

Variations: airc-luachra, arc-luachra, alt-pluachra, art-luachra, darklooker, dochi-luachair, joint-eater, just-halver, mankeeper

I witnessed a bean leighis (woman of healing) cure this poor wretch of his alp-luachra infestation near a river in Killorglin, Co. Kerry.

The alp-luachra is a small creature similar to the smooth newt (*Lissotriton vulgaris*), a harmless denizen of Irish ponds. The alp-luachra, on the other hand, is a parasitical faery that feeds not on food itself, but, according to the Reverend Robert Kirk[2], on the 'pith or quintessence' of food. Those who fall asleep by a pond or stream are most at risk of infestation, as tiny alp-luachras slip into the sleeper's open mouth and work their way to the stomach.

The host is unaware of their vile new occupants until they are overcome with an insatiable hunger as the alp-luachras ingest half their victim's food, growing larger while the host wastes away. The parasites reproduce, causing unbearable pain. The poor victim will, without intervention, starve to death within a year, whereupon the alp-luachras leave the host to search for new prey.

Douglas Hyde[3] recounts the story of a wealthy Connacht farmer who suffered badly from an alp-luachra infestation for half a year after falling asleep near a brook. Having spent most of his wealth on three ineffectual doctors, a wandering boccuch (beggarman) advised him that he had fallen foul of the 'alt-pluachra', as he called it. He insisted that he needed the help of a man called Mac Dermott, the Prince of Coolavin, who dwelt near Lough Gara in Co. Sligo.

He was taken to see the Prince, who fed the emaciated farmer a quantity of salted beef and bid him lie by a stream with his mouth open. The alp-luachras, driven to great thirst by the beef, wriggled their way from the man's stomach to his tongue and one by one plopped into the water of the stream, a dozen in all. Then the mother, seven times the size of one of her brood, came out of him as well, whereupon the farmer declared, 'I'm a new man.'

An adult alp-luachra. Olive black and speckled, with orange underbelly. Measures from ¼" up to 18" long when fully grown.

The alp-luachra lives near where a certain herb – possibly crowfoot – grows. It may reside in féar gortach or 'hungry grass', a patch of land cursed by the sidhe to cause insatiable hunger if stood upon, but this is not known for sure.

NOTES

Category: Faery beast
Lifespan: Up to 14 years
Habitat: Lakes, streams, brooks, ponds and rivers
Location: All over Ireland
Powers: Once outside the body, the alp-luachra can be licked to cure burns.

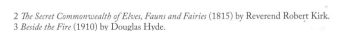

2 *The Secret Commonwealth of Elves, Fauns and Fairies* (1815) by Reverend Robert Kirk.
3 *Beside the Fire* (1910) by Douglas Hyde.

AMADÁN

'FOOL'

*Variations: amadáin mhóra, amadan dubh, amadán mór,
amadan-na-breena, amadán-na-bríona, Fool of the Forth*

*This amadán dubh tried to bewitch me with his reed pipes one midsummer eve near Lisdoonvarna, Co. Clare. However, I
had stoppered up my ears with candle wax just in case this would happen, knowing that this particular night was when the
dark fool of the faery realm was most active. I made off across the fields as fast as I could.*

The faerie realm is ruled by a nobility known as the Daoine Sidhe (People of the Hollow Hills), said to be descendants of the Tuatha Dé Danann, who were worshipped as gods by the ancient Irish. Like any royal court, the Daoine Sidhe have their own jester or fool, known as the amadán. An encounter with him can have dire consequences, especially in the month of June when his powers are at their height. The amadán's sense of humour is dark and cruel indeed, for his idea of a joke is to cause terrible ailments in humans, from addled wits to debilitating, incurable strokes. As the saying goes, there's nothing funny about a clown at midnight.[4]

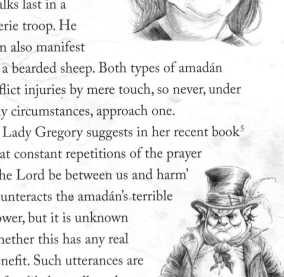

There are two types of amadán, both very dangerous. The first is the amadán dubh (dark fool), whose music will ensnare a human and drive them mad. The second kind is the amadán-na-briona (the stroke lad or white fool), a shape-shifter sometimes seen as a little fat man with a tall hat and a red scarf who always walks last in a faerie troop. He can also manifest as a bearded sheep. Both types of amadán inflict injuries by mere touch, so never, under any circumstances, approach one.

Lady Gregory suggests in her recent book[5] that constant repetitions of the prayer 'The Lord be between us and harm' counteracts the amadán's terrible power, but it is unknown whether this has any real benefit. Such utterances are in fact likely to allow the amadán to venture closer to its victim and cause 'the faerie stroke'.

Top right: A victim of an amadán. This person was unable to speak except in a garbled fashion, nor could she move her arms. She had been perfectly fit and healthy before her encounter.
Above left and right: The amadán-na-briona in his various guises.

NOTES
Category: Solitary faery
Lifespan: Unknown
Habitat: Faerie mounds
Location: All over Ireland, particularly the west.
Powers: Shape-shifter, mesmerises with music, can cause strokes in humans. Even Biddy Early, the renowned bean feasa (wise woman) of Co. Clare, was unable to heal the amadán's victims.

4 The only saying like this I could find is attributed to the horror actor Lon Chaney (1883–1930): 'A clown is funny in the circus ring. But what would be the normal reaction to opening a door at midnight, and finding the same clown standing there in the moonlight?'
5 *Visions and Beliefs in the West of Ireland* (1920) by Lady Isabella Augusta Gregory.

AUGHISKY

'WATER-HORSE'

Variations: alastyn, each uisce

Appearing as a tame horse, the aughisky will gallop out of the ocean surf at night, hunting for unwary travellers. It will attempt to ingratiate itself with a human, encouraging him to mount it, whereupon it plunges into the waves, drowns him and devours everything except his liver. This may be because the liver is toxic to the creature. As long as the aughisky stays away from salt water there is no danger, and indeed it will make a fine mount, but any sight or scent of the sea spells certain doom.

The aughisky is much like the pooka, luring travellers onto its back to take them for a wild ride. However, while the pooka is playful about the business, the aughisky is carnivorous and will certainly eat his passenger. Also, the pooka can take various forms, whereas the aughisky usually appears either as a black horse with sunken eyes, two rows of pointed teeth and seal-like skin or as a human with horselike ears. The aughisky exudes a strong adhesive from its hide as soon as it is touched by a human. It will also eat cattle, so a herd grazing near salt water should be rigorously guarded. It's nigh impossible to kill an aughisky, though if you could snare one and hold it over a fire (good luck with that!), it will melt away into a puddle of slime. Some legends say all Irish lakes are melted aughisky carcasses, but I'm not sure I believe that.

One evening in Doohooma, Co. Mayo, a young man burst into the inn where I was having a pint with three of my cousins. He breathlessly told us that his best friend had been ensnared by a wild, black horse and dragged into the ocean. The young man lead us to the lonely cove where he and his friend had been lobster fishing and we began to search the area. After half an hour or so, we spotted the beast standing in a rock pool, nuzzling at something in the water. We ran towards it, and it bolted away into the sea. In the pool we found a broken lobster pot, remnants of clothing and a liver, entirely intact, floating eerily on the surface.

The young man was questioned for many hours by the Garda Síochána on suspicion of killing his friend, but was released with no charges. The rumours and stigma remained for years after, when all he was guilty of was fishing for lobster to sell at sixpence a pound.

NOTES

Category: Faery water beast

Lifespan: 25–30 years

Habitat: Aughiska[6] are nocturnal, solitary saltwater creatures, claiming long coastal territories. They venture out mostly in November, but can be encountered at other times of the year.

Location: All over Irish coastlines. Some tamed aughiska reside inland. There are unconfirmed reports of sightings in some lakes.

Powers: The aughisky is an amphibious creature with some kind of natural adhesive on its skin, similar to barnacle cement. Some say strong alcohol will dissolve the adhesive, but it would be a dextrous man who could pour whiskey whilst being dragged into the sea.

See also: Pooka

6 Evidently 'aughiska' is the plural form.

BANSHEE

'WOMAN OF THE FAERIES'

Variations: banshie, ban side, bean sí, bean-síghe, ben síde, sí-bhean

A banshee I saw sitting amongst the rushes of the Camogue River, Co. Tipperary. She spotted me, then disappeared into a white mist with a sound not unlike the flapping of bird wings. I found her comb at the spot.

Of all the creatures of Irish folklore, the banshee is probably the most misunderstood. Many mortals live in terror of her wail, fearing it means she has come to claim their soul. Nothing could be further from the truth. Banshees do not cause death; they forewarn of it, giving a family who hear her cries time to prepare for the demise of a loved one.

Until recently, when a death occurred in Ireland, professional mourners were often hired to lead the lamentations for the deceased. This practice was called keening – a high-pitched, ululating wail, which raises one's hackles – from the Irish word 'caoineadh', meaning to cry or weep. This is the terrible sound that witnesses of the banshee often hear. However, the banshee keens for the victim *before* they shuffle off their mortal coil.

It is said that the banshee cries only for ancient Irish noble families with an Ó or Mac in their name, but of late her shriek has been less discriminating and all manner of people, including families of Norse, Norman and Anglo-Saxon descent, have heard and even seen her. Indeed, in the seventeenth century, a Lady Fanshawe recounts in her memoirs[7] how she was awakened in the night at Lady Honora O'Brien's castle in Co. Galway by a red-haired spirit. With a 'ghastly complexion', lit by the moon, it cried, 'Ahone, Ahone, Ahone' ('Alas! Alas! Alas!'),

before fading away with a sigh 'more like wind than breath'. It was discovered the next morning that a cousin of Lady O'Brien's had died in another part of the castle.

A banshee can take on many forms, but the most commonly witnessed is that of an old woman with long, flowing white hair. She has also been seen as a beautiful young woman wearing a death shroud, a pale woman in a white dress with long red hair and even a headless woman carrying a bowl of blood. One common feature is that the banshee's eyes are roaring red, caused by constant crying. Remember, if you should you hear or see a banshee, it does not necessarily mean you yourself will die. But someone in the vicinity certainly will.

I put the banshee's comb here, but it has since vanished, to where I know not. Perhaps its owner came in the night and reclaimed it.

NOTES

Category: Solitary faery
Lifespan: Immortal
Habitat: Inhabits the Otherworld, manifesting on this earthly plane in lonely places, often near water.
Location: All over Ireland and even sometimes in foreign countries to which Irish people have emigrated.
Powers: Foreknowledge of death. Has a keening wail that can carry for miles. Can shape-shift into a hare, stoat or hooded crow.
See also: Dullahan

7 *The Memoirs of Ann, Lady Fanshawe, Wife of the Right Honble. Sir Richard Fanshawe, Bart., 1600–72* (1676) by Lady Ann Harrison Fanshawe.

CAILLEACH

'HOODED ONE'

Variations: cailleach bhéara, cailleach feasa, cailleach phiseogach, calaigh bherra, cally berry, clooth na Bare, garavogue, hag of Beara, Queen of Winter

The cailleach is an ancient weather deity who rules the winter half of the year, from Samhain to Bealtaine[8], with the goddess Bríghde ruling the summer half. Some legends state that she becomes younger as winter goes on and transforms into the beautiful, youthful personification of spring. It's said her grandchildren and great-grandchildren are the people and races of Ireland. It's not known how old she is, but some estimates put her as ancient as creation itself.

I met this cowled crone with one eye and deathly pale skin on the summit of Slieve Gullion, Co. Armagh, early one May Day. We passed each other on the path and when I turned to look at her again, she was nowhere to be seen. But there was this pile of rocks I was certain had not been there before.

One legend has it that Fintan mac Bóchra, he of the hundred lives, accompanied Noah's granddaughter Cessair to Ireland before the great flood. He thought himself the first to set foot on the island, but found the cailleach already living there, and saw she was far older than he – a slip of a lad at a mere 5,500 years.

There's a well-known tale of a travelling friar and his scribe who happened upon the cottage of the cailleach. Despite it being considered impolite to ask a woman her age, the friar did so. She told him that she killed a beef cow once a year and threw the bones up into the loft. 'If you wish to know my age, send your boy up on the loft to count the bones.' The scribe spent the better part of the day counting the bones and still hadn't gotten through the ones in a single corner of the loft.[9]

The cailleach is associated with numerous places in Ireland, from the Hag's Head on the Cliffs of Moher in Co. Clare to the desolate Wailing Woman rock on Skellig Michael, Co. Kerry. Despite her years, she can make great leaps across the land, spilling boulders from her apron to form hills and mountains, like Slieve na Calliagh in Co. Meath.

On the first day of February, the cailleach gathers firewood. If the weather is fine that day, it is said she will be able to gather plenty of dry wood for her fire and winter will last for some time yet. If the weather is foul that day, the cailleach stays asleep; she will soon run out of wood and winter is almost over. At Bealtaine, the cailleach casts her staff away under a holly or gorse bush and turns to stone, which remains moist throughout summer because of the life force it contains.

The cailleach is also the goddess of the harvest. Whatever crops are not taken in by the end of October must be left as a tithe to her, and will poison the mortal who eats of them. In parts of Ireland, the corn dolly[10] is still made as an offering to her.

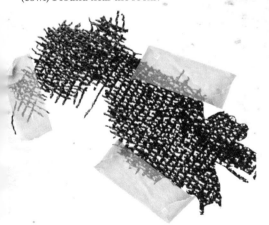

A fragment of the cailleach bhéara's cochall (cowl) I found near the rocks.

NOTES
Category: Deity
Lifespan: Immortal
Habitat: Craggy mountains
Location: Mainly counties Armagh, Clare, Cork, Galway, Kerry, Meath and Sligo
Powers: Shape-shifting, weather and wind manipulation. Able to make great leaps. Cares for animals during winter.

8 Samhain is what we now call Halloween; Bealtaine is what we now call May Day.
9 *Legends of Saints and Sinners* (1915) by Douglas Hyde.
10 This ancient tradition involves weaving corn from the last standing sheaf in a field. As a symbol of life it couldn't be more apt, looking ostensibly like spirals of DNA.

CHANGELING

Variations: fágálach, iarlais, malartán, síofra

Throughout the entirety of Irish history, there are countless reports of faerie abductions. Even notable personages like the mythical high king Cormac mac Airt and Cú Chulainn himself were lured away to the Otherworld[11]. As recently as 1895, Michael Cleary, a cooper from Co. Tipperary, gave as the motive for killing his wife Bridget that she had been taken by the faeries and replaced with a changeling[12].

The question is, why would faeries want to abduct a human?

I was asked by friends in Castleblayney, Co. Monaghan, to identify whether their precious infant son had been taken by the faeries. One look in the crib told me that indeed he had. I made a charm from old horseshoe nails, hen excrement and salt that scared away the changeling[13]. My friends' son was waiting for them by their back door the following morning. I advised them to put iron tongs in the baby's cradle to prevent it from happening again, for faeries hate iron. Flowers, especially primroses, spread on windowsills or hung on door-posts and red berries from holly, rowan and ash trees will protect the home and keep faeries at bay. Herbs such as St John's wort and yarrow also offer potent protection against faeries.

It's said that the blood of faeries is white, which may explain their pale, almost translucent complexions. It's possible that faeries wish to intermarry with humans to bolster their bloodlines with red human blood. European royal families occasionally act this way, allowing an outsider into the fold to genetically diversify their bloodline. Other, more prosaic reasons for the abduction of human adults may include the faeries' need for servants, midwives or wet nurses, for some say that weak faerie children require human milk to survive. Some adults return after several years, much changed, but many do not. In many cases, a changeling or a stock[14] is left that looks exactly like the abductee. At least at first.

Many faerie children perish before birth and of those that survive, some are stunted or deformed. A grieving faery mother, or a father who is dissatisfied with his progeny, may abduct a human baby or employ the services of a 'fear dearg', an expert in such things. Their prey may be a child who has not yet been baptised or one who is excessively admired.

Changelings include actual faery children and wizened, senile old faeries. The former is harder to spot and might even grow up in a household without the family realising it is a simulacrum of their loved one. The child may be scrawny and sickly, but exhibit a precocious nature along with faerie traits such as mischievousness, general oddness and an aptitude for music. The old faery changeling disguised as a baby or toddler will display characteristics such as a foul temper, dark and deep-set eyes, facial hair, a full set of teeth (oft-times sharp), a ravenous appetite (it may also demand strong liquor) and jaundiced or wizened skin. Naturally, these are easier to identify.

One woman who was convinced her child had been stolen tricked the faery into revealing its true nature by boiling eggshells. The infant laughed and said in a gruff voice, 'I'm fifteen hundred years in the world, and I never saw a brewery of egg-shells before!'[15] Once a changeling has been outed, the stolen child is usually returned.

---

11 The Otherworld is the realm of the faeries, also known by other names such as Tír na nÓg (Land of the Young), Mag Mell (Plain of Delight) and Tír Tairngire (Land of Promise).
12 Michael Cleary was found guilty of manslaughter and sentenced to 20 years' penal servitude. He spent 15 years in prison and later emigrated to Canada.
13 Unfortunately, other lethal methods have been employed in the past such as beating, burning and torture.
14 A stock is usually an inanimate object, such as a piece of wood, that has a spell cast upon it to resemble the abducted person. The stock would soon grow very ill and waste away like rotting timber.
15 *Fairy Legends and Traditions of the South of Ireland* (1825) by Thomas Crofton Croker.

NOTES

Category: Solitary faery

Lifespan: Unknown

Habitat: In homes everywhere

Location: All over Ireland

Powers: Wisdom beyond its apparent years

See also: Fear dearg

CLURICHAUN

'CHATTER-HEAD'

Variations: clobhair-cheann, cluracan, cluracaun, cluricaun, cluricaune

The average leprechaun would say different, but he is a close relative of the roguish clurichaun. To say this creature likes a bit of a drink would be rather understating the matter. He spends most of his time haunting well-stocked wine cellars and will imbibe at every opportunity. Some say the clurichaun is just a drunk leprechaun, rather than a different species, but I would say otherwise, as the clurichaun is a gifted wordsmith who loves nothing more than sharing a wee drop of whiskey with a friendly ear in exchange for

Whilst crossing a field near Tarmonbarry, Co. Roscommon, one night, I spotted this drunken clurichaun riding on the back of a farm dog. He was unaware of me and I drew this sketch at my leisure by the light of the moon.

wonderful tales. Hence the meaning of his name: chatter-head.

Like his cousin the leprechaun, he can range from six inches to three feet tall, and he likes to wear red, though he dresses very slovenly. He has twinkling eyes, a face like a withered apple, an unkempt beard and a bulbous nose that's purple from drinking.

So does this drunken wee eejit have any redeeming qualities? Well, if you keep a decent amount of good quality booze in your cellar, he will guard it with his life. Despite his troublesome nature, he will take special care of a family to whom he attaches himself. He will protect them and their property as long as he is not interfered with.

He is a mischievous practical joker, and when he's had a little too much, he can be as mean as a snake. He will exact a terrible revenge if he feels slighted, which he often

does. Not keeping a decent supply of alcohol, leaving him out the wrong kind of food and being dishonest are but a few of the reasons why a clurichaun might start acting the maggot in your home. And like every drunk, he can be hard to get rid of.

The clurichaun can often be seen at two or three in the morning riding on the backs of farm dogs or tormenting sheep. Garlands of marsh marigolds hung over barn doors will prevent clurichauns from entering and stealing farm animals for these nocturnal joyrides.

It is said he carries a purse or a pewter cup with a 'spre na skillenagh' (lucky shilling) in it that always returns to its owner. Many a mortal has tried without success to seize a clurichaun for his purse. Even when captured, he can vanish if his captor looks away for the briefest moment. A bit like a drunk whose round it is in the pub.

The landlord of an establishment I visited in Crossmolina, Co. Mayo, gave me (or rather sold me for several times its actual value) this coin he claimed he got from a clurichaun he had captured. Apparently, the clurichaun carried two purses: one contained the magic shilling and the other a normal copper coin. He gave the landlord the latter before disappearing.

NOTES

Category: Solitary faery

Lifespan: Unknown

Habitat: Wine cellars of big houses, pub cellars

Location: Mainly the province of Munster. WB Yeats states the clurichaun is 'almost unknown in Connaught and the north'.[16]

Powers: Can drink most mortals under the table. Marvellous story-teller. Can transform bog rushes into a horse to use as a mount. Vanishes as soon as you take your eyes off him.

See also: Leprechaun

16 *Fairy and Folk Tales of the Irish Peasantry* (1888) by WB Yeats.

THE DEVIL

Variations: Beelzebub, Himself, Lord of the Flies, Lucifer, Old Nick, Satan, The Divil,
The Horned One

There are many Irish tales and songs involving the Devil. He is usually presented as more of a trickster figure, like the god Loki from Norse mythology, than the Biblical personification of evil. But if you subscribe to the theory that faeries are the rebellious angels who were cast out of Heaven, then Satan is the absolute King of the Faeries. In many European traditions, the Devil is the leader of the Wild Hunt, known as 'sluagh na marbh' in Ireland – a deadly flock of leathery-winged faeries who steal human souls.

I spotted Himself making a deal with some poor fool in the lobby of a swanky hotel in Dublin city. I could easily perceive his dark aura, and he knew I knew who he was, for he winked at me before placing a well-manicured finger at the spot where the wretch was to sign away his soul – in his own blood, of course.

In Irish tales, the Devil is commonly outwitted or entrapped in some clever way by a roguish Irishman, though the rogue doesn't always escape scot-free. The folk tale of Stingy Jack ends with the eponymous hero wandering 'twixt worlds forever, with only a coal from Hell's infernal flames to light his way. There's another tale of an Irishman with three sons who makes a bargain with Satan. When the time comes to pay up, he asks the Devil if he will hold off claiming his soul until the candle on his table has burned down to the stub. The Devil, seeing there isn't much life left in the candle, obligingly agrees, whereupon one of the man's quick-witted sons blows out the candle and slips it into his pocket.

Some tales involve the vice of gambling, such as the one of several dandies playing cards with an enigmatic stranger in the notorious Hellfire Club in the Dublin mountains[17]. One of the men drops a card, reaches down for it under the table and sees that the stranger's feet are cloven hooves. Variations of this tale abound in Ireland, including one set in Loftus Hall on the Hook peninsula in Co. Wexford, reputed to be Ireland's most haunted house. Lady Anne Tottenham saw the stranger's hooves, whereupon the Devil 'vanished in a thunder-clap leaving a brimstone smell behind him.'[18] Lady Anne went insane and died shortly after, and her shade is said to haunt the place. All that being said, 'It may be that this, like the others, was not the devil at all, but some poor wood spirit whose cloven feet had got him into trouble.'[19]

One story tells of the Devil making a deal with a tailor, saying he would come to collect his soul in twelve months' time. Satan told him, 'If ye have a job that I am not able to do then ye won't have to come with me.' When the fated day arrived, the tailor broke wind loudly and said, 'Sew a button on that!'

Thankfully I've not had occasion to make any kind of deal with Old Nick myself, for I'm not sure I have the wily tongue, cunning legal brain or intestinal gases required to outfox him. He appears in a variety of guises, but these days is likely to sport the attire of a suave businessman, sans hooves.

---

17 Originally an ancient cairn stood at the top of Montpelier Hill, Co. Dublin. In 1725, wealthy politician William 'Speaker' Conolly allegedly destroyed the cairn and built a hunting lodge in its place, using a stone from the cairn as the lintel of his fireplace. Shortly after, Conolly died. In 1735, the lodge was bought by the aristocrat Richard Parsons, an occultist and black magician, who founded the Irish Hellfire Club there. All sorts of depravity, both natural and preternatural, are reported to have occurred at the Club, whose members Jonathan Swift called 'a brace of monsters, blasphemers and bacchanalians'. It now lies in ruins.
18 *True Irish Ghost Stories* (1914) compiled by St John D Seymour and Harry L Neligan.
19 *The Celtic Twilight* (1893) by WB Yeats.

NOTES

Category: Fallen angel

Lifespan: Immortal

Habitat: Hell

Location: Underground

Powers: Practically limitless power. Shape-shifter. Snappy dresser. Expert in legalese, especially having been thwarted so many times over the years by crafty Irishmen. His more recent contracts contain multitudes of clauses and small print.

See also: Sluagh na marbh

DOBHAR-CHÚ

'WATER-HOUND'

Variations: anchu, dhuragoo, dobarcu, dorraghowor, doyarchu,
Irish crocodile, King Otter, Master Otter

My attempt at capturing the dobhar-chú's furious lightning attack. Note the white, almost albino fur, the distinctive cross shape on its back and the webbed toes.

Although the Irish word for otter is 'dobharchú', and eyewitnesses have described this ferocious denizen of Irish waters as otter-like, here the similarities between the common otter (*Lutra lutra*) and the monstrous dobhar-chú end. Tales of this gigantic, carnivorous creature with a taste for human flesh have been recounted in Ireland since ancient times and there have been many modern sightings. They often hunt in pairs or small groups, and give off an eerie, high-pitched whistle when about to die, to warn their mate.

Roderic O'Flaherty[20] reported one man's terrifying encounter with what he called the 'Irish crocodil' on the shore of Lough Mask in Co. Mayo. The creature, described as about the size of a greyhound, with slimy black skin, dragged the man into the lake. The man managed to stab the creature with his pocket-knife, scaring it away.

More recently, a Miss LA Walkington[21] told of an animal that was either an 'enormous sea-otter' or was 'half-wolfdog and half-fish'. Apparently, a young woman was washing clothes in a river near Glenade Lough, Co. Leitrim, when she was attacked by a 'dhuragoo'. Her husband heard her screams and ran to her aid, but she was already dead, with the monster 'sucking her blood'. A gravestone in a cemetery in Conwall, Co. Leitrim, dated September 1722, has an engraving of the dobhar-chú and is said to be the poor woman's grave.

Perhaps foolishly, myself and a fellow researcher tracked dobhar-chú spraints (dung) around the shores of Lough Maumeenmaunragh in Co. Galway. Unlike the almost fragrant odour of ordinary otter droppings, this spraint smelled rather like rotting flesh. It contained bones of many small animals, such as rabbits and birds. We followed the grisly trail throughout the afternoon, the stench getting stronger, until we spotted a dobhar-chú on the eastern side of the lough. Through my spyglass, its sleek, round head and black ear tips were just visible above the waterline, slipping silently towards a group of wild red deer slaking their thirst. It lunged out of the water, its slim body easily fifteen feet in length, and snatched one of the deer in its maw. The unfortunate creature was dragged down into the lough, which churned and roiled as the dobhar-chú rolled its prey around in the reddening water. Then it was gone into the depths, leaving nothing but the still, glassy surface of the lough and startled deer bounding away through the heather.

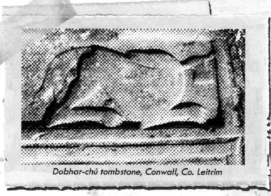

Dobhar-chú tombstone, Conwall, Co. Leitrim

NOTES

Category: Rare water beast

Lifespan: Unknown. Mortal, for it is said it can be killed by a silver bullet, though the killer will die within a day himself.

Habitat: Freshwater rivers and loughs; sometimes the coast

Location: All over Ireland, but largely in the west, particularly in and around Sraheens Lough, Achill Island, Co. Mayo. Possibly a migratory species, living in Ireland only part of the year.

Powers: Travels at incredible speeds, in or out of water. Powerful bite. A cutting from its pelt is believed to prevent a ship from wrecking, a horse from drowning or a man from being injured by gunshot.

20 *A Chorographical Description of West or H-Iar Connaught* (1684) by Roderic O'Flaherty.
21 *The Journal of the Royal Society of Antiquaries of Ireland* (1896).

DULLAHAN

'WITHOUT A HEAD'

Variations: Crom Dubh, dulachan, dullaghan, durahan, fear dorcha, gan cheann

I beheld this dullahan one night near Kilcoo, Co. Down.
Upon hearing the thunder of wheels, I hid behind a bush and
covered my ears until the dreadful phantasm had passed, lest the name
he called was my own. I later heard a young woman in the village had died
suddenly, shortly after I witnessed the apparition.

If it's your name the dullahan calls out from the awful, slitted mouth of the head he carries (presumably his own, but who knows?), your soul will be sucked right out of you and you'll drop dead on the spot. The head has mouldy cheese-coloured skin and is luminescent somehow, as the dullahan has been witnessed holding it aloft to light his way on moonless nights. He can see long distances with two darting, piggy eyes, which fix upon the house of the person he then goes to fetch.

The dullahan haunts dark and lonely roads. Should you happen to gaze upon this terrifying phantom as he passes by your window, he will either strike you blind in one eye or throw a vessel of blood in your face, according to WB Yeats.[22]

In most accounts, the dullahan rides a ferocious black steed that breathes fire, and he beats the beast not with a whip but with a human spine. Sometimes though, he rides in a black death coach (cóiste bodhar or coach-a-bower), which has thigh bones for wheel spokes and candles in skulls to light the way. It is covered in human skin leather or worm-eaten funeral pall. The coach is so fast that sparks from its wheels set the trees and brush along the road alight, and no gate can withstand its onslaught. So unless you're blind, deaf or completely witless, you're definitely going to behold the dullahan coming for you, despite cóiste bodhar meaning 'silent coach'.

There are myriad Irish tales of people hearing the rumble of the cóiste bodhar's wheels in the blackness of night along with the wailing of the banshee, whom the dullahan sometimes accompanies.

The dullahan's origins are shrouded in mystery, but he does have a dubious association with the ancient Irish fertility god Crom Dubh, who demanded human sacrifices every year, usually by decapitation. It's said that once Christianity put a stop to the pagan practice of sacrifice, Crom took on the physical embodiment of the dullahan and continued his soul-stealing in this headless form.

Can anything stop this terrifying phantasm? Well, unlike mortal undertakers, the dullahan is not fond of gold, so it's probably a good idea to carry a gold coin or two in your pocket to dissuade him from pilfering your soul.

A gold sovereign for dullahan-related emergencies.

NOTES

Category: Solitary faery

Lifespan: Unknown

Habitat: Dark, lonely roads

Location: Mainly counties Down and Sligo

Powers: Able to see over great distances and traverse them quickly.

See also: Banshee

22 *Fairy and Folk Tales of the Irish Peasantry* (1888) by WB Yeats.

FEAR DEARG

'RED MAN'

Variations: far darrig, fir darrig, fir dhearga, rat boy

A sketch of the fear dearg I met on the towpath of the Royal Canal, near Maynooth, Co. Kildare. I could smell him coming before I could see him. Despite his dishevelled appearance and breath so bad you could cut it with a knife, I was careful to be polite, and shared my sandwiches with him, which he disgustingly devoured within seconds. In return, he regaled me with stories of his wild youth as a human. I couldn't tell if he was being truthful or not, but he certainly liked to hear himself talk. That night I had awful dreams that I cannot bring myself to speak of, even today.

The fear dearg is the vagrant of the faerie world, most often seen wearing a battered hat or raggedy cap and an old, red coat you wouldn't use to patch a flour sack. He is an obese, rat-faced little man with dark, hairy skin, wild red or grey hair and a straggly, unkempt beard. In some parts of the country, such as Donegal, he is described as being very tall. In Munster, he is only two and a half feet tall. Sometimes he is described as having a rat's tail. He often carries a shillelagh – a blackthorn walking stick – topped with the skull of some unfortunate creature or other.

Despite all this, if you can swallow your disgust and engage in conversation with him, he will sometimes impart useful information about the faerie realm, usually on how to avoid it altogether, but also how to escape it if you become trapped there. This advice should be taken with a pinch of salt, for some fir dearg[23] may have been human once and become trapped in the faerie realm, so they may not be the greatest authorities on the subject. Like other solitary faeries, the fear dearg is 'most sluttish, slouching, jeering, mischievous'[24] and generally not to be trusted.

I've heard that the first thing you must say upon meeting a fear dearg is, 'Ná bí ag magadh fúm!' or, 'Do not mock me!' It's said this utterance will counteract the fear dearg's evil pishogue[25], but in reality it is likely only to get his back up.

The fear dearg likes to make mischief by kidnapping people and holding them against their will for days on end and 'busies himself with practical joking, especially with gruesome joking. This he does, and nothing else.'[26] Some accounts state he sets traps for humans then drags them away in a burlap sack to his bog hut and forces them to make him dinner from a hag skewered on a spit over a fire! This is likely to be fearful exaggeration, for he's not a fussy eater and would eat uncooked flesh, being especially fond of rotting fish and carrion.

Some fir dearg do the dirty work of barren faeries who wish to raise a human child, for it's said he 'steals children from their cradles, and leaves sickly elves in their places'[27]. For this reason, you should be on your guard when a fear dearg lets himself into your house and warms himself by your fire. It is better to let him do this than to chase him, but always use sensible precautions, such as leaving iron tongs in your baby's crib, for faeries cannot abide iron.

---

23 The plural form of 'fear' (man) is 'fir' (men) in Irish.
24 *Fairy and Folk Tales of the Irish Peasantry* (1888) by WB Yeats.
25 A pishogue is a faerie spell or magic, comparable to fairy 'glamour' in Britain.
26 Yeats (1888) *ibid.*
27 *The Dead-watchers, And Other Folk-lore Tales Of Westmeath* (1891) by Patrick Bardan.

NOTES

Category: Solitary faery

Lifespan: Unknown. They could well be mortal.

Habitat: Swamps, marshes, middens, cess pits, riverbanks, canals, sewers, polluted coastlines and coastal ruins. Most active in winter.

Location: All over Ireland, particularly near the coast.

Powers: Causes bad dreams, expert at swapping changelings.

See also: Changeling

FEAR GORTA

'MAN OF HUNGER'

Variations: fair-gortha, far gorta, fear-gerta

I was a boy of nine when visiting relatives at Bunnacranna, Co. Sligo. We had heard they were suffering the effects of 'an Gorta Beag' (mini-famine)[28] and me, my father, my brother Ferdia and sister Fionnuala had brought some provisions to tide them over. On the same evening as the Virgin Mary visited Knock[29], less than twenty miles away, this fear gorta appeared to us at the back door of my aunt and uncle's house. My aunt gave him some bread, beef and a few coins and he went away. Not long after, our relatives' fortunes changed for the better.

Is there a more woeful creature in all of Irish folklore than the fear gorta? This solitary faery wanders the lonely roads of Ireland as an emaciated, rag-draped wretch, begging for alms. His skin has a sickly green tint to it and his stick-thin arms can barely hold his begging bowl, in which a single coin rattles.

Despite his frightful appearance, the fear gorta can reward generosity with good fortune, but will curse those that spurn him with rotten luck. So it's advisable always to be kind should you encounter a fear gorta on a pitch-black road at night, even if your own provisions are meagre and the sight of him makes you want to turn on your heel.

Some say he is the ghost of someone who died of famine or a wraith from the Otherworld. Others maintain that he is a harbinger of hard times to come. The origin of this sorry creature is rooted in Ireland's ancient past, when famines were a common occurrence and sacrifices had to be made to placate the gods. There was even a Celtic tradition called the threefold death, where a king was sacrificed if the crops failed. He was drowned, hanged and stabbed and his body offered to the gods of old, the Tuatha Dé Danann, to invoke a successful harvest for the coming season.

More recently, the Great Hunger[30] saw many poor, starving Irish folk wandering the roads, their lips stained green from the grass they were forced to eat. The fear gorta's green-tinged skin could be a reminder of that dreadful time – perhaps the creature is a personification of famine itself, made manifest by faerie magic.

Over time, the fear gorta has become conflated with the féar gortach or 'hungry grass', simply because the Irish word for man is 'fear' and for grass, 'féar'. Féar gortach, a patch of land cursed by the sidhe, can cause insatiable hunger if stood upon, but it is not associated with the fear gorta other than the similarity of the name. It is possible that hungry grass is the habitat for a faery creature called the alp-luachra, though this is my own hypothesis.

NOTES

Category: Solitary faery
Lifespan: Unknown
Habitat: Lonely roadsides
Location: Mainly the west and southern regions of Ireland.
Powers: Able to grant good luck if given food and bad luck if spurned.
See also: Alp-luachra

28 The so-called 'mini-famine' or 'forgotten famine' of 1879 was the last main Irish famine and was concentrated mostly in the west of Ireland.
29 An apparition of the Virgin Mary is said to have appeared to multiple witnesses at the village of Knock, Co. Mayo, on 21 August 1879.
30 The Great Famine or Great Hunger (*an Gorta Mór*) was a period of starvation and disease, mainly in the west and south of Ireland, lasting from 1845 to 1852. It is estimated around one million people died of starvation and another million fled the country.

FEAR LIATH

'GREY MAN'

Variations: brolaghan, far liath, an fir lea, Old Boneless

I saw this terrifying fear liath striding towards me as I sat enjoying the fine weather at The Gobbins cliffs at Islandmagee, Co. Antrim. Within moments, the sun was gone and the fear liath had engulfed the entire coastline. For hours the village was oppressed by a sodden, claggy[31] gloom that penetrated the bones.

Some say the fear liath is the modern-day form of an ancient storm or weather deity, worshipped by coastal inhabitants thousands of years ago. Others say he is a solitary faery with a malignant bent. In either case, he hates humans and delights in causing mayhem and death among mortals. Composed entirely of mist and fog, there is hardly any physical substance to him, which is why he is called Old Boneless in the west of Ireland.

In some places, like counties Cork and Kerry, he is the size of a man, but in Wexford and Waterford he appears as little more than a ragged, hazy shadow that leaves a trail of mist behind. In counties Antrim and Down, he is a gigantic humanoid and is known as a brolaghan, meaning 'a formless or shapeless thing'. This discrepancy of size is likely ascribable to the dynamic nature of coastal mists, which can appear very suddenly on the horizon before growing larger and sweeping in to plunge the land into blind chaos.

The fear liath often uses his 'grey man's breath' to conceal rocks, causing ships to sink or travellers to fall to their deaths. His touch can sour milk, blight potatoes, cause clothes to become permanently damp and render peat so wet as to be unburnable. In some places, his cloak causes sicknesses like sore throats and influenza.

He can feed on chimney smoke, and so is sometimes found in urban areas, where his cloak stinks of mould and woodsmoke. For this reason, I think the fear liath is not a type of faery, for faeries cannot abide smoke and they avoid towns and cities whenever possible.

Boats can be protected by having a blessed silver coin or medal embedded in the prow. Holy water sprinkled over foodstuffs will protect them from his foul touch.

A natural phenomenon known as a 'mountain spectre' [32] can occur in certain atmospheric conditions. One's own enormously magnified shadow can be cast onto a bank of cloud, creating the illusion of a gigantic figure in the air, but the fear liath is most certainly not this. Shadows don't kill innocent travellers.

Grey Man's Path, Fairhead, Ballycastle

A postcard showing the Grey Man's Path in Co. Antrim. Locals will go out of their way to avoid it, especially if the weather has taken a turn for the worse, lest the fear liath leads them onto the rocks far below.

NOTES

Category: Solitary faery or deity

Lifespan: Possibly immortal

Habitat: Mostly coastal regions, but also manifests on hills, mountaintops and boggy hollows. Appears most often at the end of autumn.

Location: North Antrim, Cork, Down, Galway, Kerry, Limerick, Sligo, Waterford, Wexford

Powers: Death and misery

31 This great word is not of Irish origin, but from North East England. It means stickily clingy, like mud. Of weather it means damp, overcast and misty.
32 Also known as a 'Brocken spectre'. Named after the German mountain on which it was first noted in 1780 by Johann Silberschlag, a German Lutheran pastor and natural scientist. The term has been mentioned in works by Samuel Taylor Coleridge, Lewis Carroll and Charles Dickens, amongst others.

FETCH

'WRAITH'

Variations: co-walker, doppelgänger, double-ganger, fáith, fylgja, wraith

I was calling on my Aunt Catherine one day when I met her son, my young cousin Niall, coming out as I was going in. I was surprised to see him, for the last I'd heard, he was fighting with the Royal Dublin Fusiliers at the Battle of the Somme. I said hello to him as he passed me in full uniform, but he said nothing. My aunt didn't mention her son's visit, and so I decided not to speak of my encounter either. Aunt Catherine received a letter ten days later stating that Niall had been killed by German machine-gun fire, around the time I met him.

'She only looked with a dead, dead eye
And a wan, wan cheek of sorrow.
I knew her Fetch; she was called to die
And she died upon the morrow.'[33]

A fetch is a supernatural double or apparition of a living person, usually seen by a family member or loved one. Accounts date back to ancient Ireland, and a sighting is regarded as an omen, usually of impending death.

It's not known why the Irish version of the Germanic doppelgänger is called a fetch. Perhaps it comes from the Irish verb 'féach' (to see), or the old Irish word for a prophet or seer, 'fáith'. It may come from the verb 'to fetch' as in 'to fetch a soul'. It is believed by some to be a kind of spirit guide, a facsimile of the doomed person to lead them into the afterlife. Who better to trust but yourself to lead you into the Great Beyond?

It is said that if the double appears in the morning rather than the evening[34], it is a sign of a long life in store, but this is not known to be true. My own fetch experience occurred in the morning.

The appearance of a fetch should not be confused with the phenomenon known as an 'arrival case'[35]. This is where a living person is seen at a location in advance of his actual arrival, thought to be some kind of projection of the person's consciousness. The fetch is not this. It is somehow a part of, but distinct from, a person's soul. It may be related to the Norse concept of the 'fylgja', a spirit being whose name means 'to accompany'.

There is also a phenomenon in Ireland known as the 'fetch-candle', a floating light that traces the route from a person's home to their grave before they die. Like the banshee, the fetch foretells of death, but does not cause it, and so should not be feared.

Cousin Niall.

NOTES
Category: Thivish
Lifespan: Unknown
Habitat: Otherworld
Location: All over Ireland
Powers: None as such, being merely an omen. It is neither good nor evil.
See also: Banshee, Sheerie

33 *The Fetch* (1825) by John Banim.
34 As related by John and Michael Banim in their story, 'The Fetches' (1867).
35 The Society for Psychical Research in London studied this phenomenon and published their findings in an exhaustive survey, *Phantasms of the Living* (1918).

GANCANAGH

'LOVE TALKER'

Variations: geancánach, gean-canagh, glanconer, gonconer

My tragic encounter with a gancanagh took place one misty morning amid the arresting beauty of Glenariff, the 'Queen of the Glens' in Co. Antrim. I was following the Dungonnell Way down the valley towards Martinstown, my heart lifted by birdsong from the trees lining the trail. Then the birdsong ceased and before long I happened upon a young man leaning languidly against a gate-post, an unlit dudeen (clay pipe) in his mouth. He had about him the look of a loodheramaun[36]– a fellow with no job of work to do, although it was a Tuesday morning in April. As I passed, his dark eyes twinkled under his hat and he leered at me. He was a slight fellow, a good head shorter than I and, although at that moment I could not discern what it was, there was something 'off' about him.

Carrying on down the trail, I noticed the birdsong had resumed. Soon I met a plump, rosy-cheeked milk-maid carrying two empty pails on a yoke over her shoulders. I cocked my cap to her and she gave a cheery smile as she robustly made her way to her morning's lactic labours. It was several minutes before my mind snapped back to what was 'off' about the youth.

I quickly turned and dashed up the twisting trail after the milk-maid. As I rounded a corner, I espied her, hunched by the gate-post where the young buck had been, weeping terribly. I cursed myself for a fool for not heeding the clues: the slender young man was clearly lazy, had cast no shadow and his pipe was not lit – sure signs of a gancanagh. Faeries hate smoke, but a gancanagh will always have an unlit dudeen in his mouth, presumably thinking it makes him look like a dandy.

Hot, salty tears rolled down the unfortunate milk-maid's ruddy cheeks. Before I asked the question, I already knew the answer: 'Did you kiss him?' She nodded, blubbering at the memory. 'I love him,' she cried, 'but how can I? I've never met him before! It was his eyes … his dark eyes and his sweet, sweet voice!' I knew this poor girl would never get over her tryst with the faery love-talker. She was doomed to pine after him, rejecting all others, eventually wasting away from a broken heart.

Fragments of the gancanagh's dudeen, which, like the milk-maid's heart, lay shattered into pieces. She gave me these and kept the rest.

*'I thought him human lover, though his lips on mine were cold,
And the breath of death blew keen on me within his hold.'*[37]

NOTES

Category: Solitary faery

Lifespan: Unknown

Habitat: Lonely valleys

Location: Mainly the northern parts of Ireland. Yeats states that the gancanagh is 'not well-known in Connacht'[38], though Ethna Carbury mentions Inisheer in Co. Galway in her poem, 'The Love-Talker'.

Powers: The gancanagh has no shadow. When he is around, birds stop singing and a mist unfurls about him. Considered very unlucky.

See also: Leanan sídhe

36 From the Irish word 'liúdramán', a loafer.
37 *The Love-Talker* (1902) by Ethna Carbery.
38 *Fairy and Folk Tales of the Irish Peasantry* (1888) by WB Yeats.

GROGOCH

'WRINKLED BROW'

Variations: grugach, laughremen

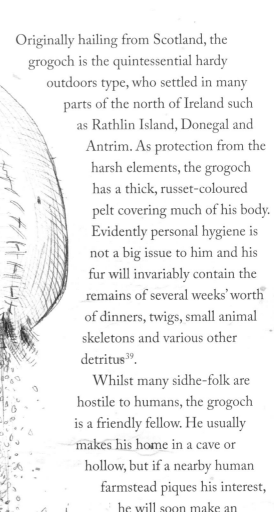

Originally hailing from Scotland, the grogoch is the quintessential hardy outdoors type, who settled in many parts of the north of Ireland such as Rathlin Island, Donegal and Antrim. As protection from the harsh elements, the grogoch has a thick, russet-coloured pelt covering much of his body. Evidently personal hygiene is not a big issue to him and his fur will invariably contain the remains of several weeks' worth of dinners, twigs, small animal skeletons and various other detritus[39].

Whilst many sidhe-folk are hostile to humans, the grogoch is a friendly fellow. He usually makes his home in a cave or hollow, but if a nearby human farmstead piques his interest, he will soon make an

A grogoch I saw 'helping out' at a farm near Ballycastle, Co. Antrim.

appearance, taking it upon himself to 'help out around the place'. Whilst this extra pair of hands may initially be useful to a farmer and his family, the grogoch will eventually get on everyone's nerves, generally getting underfoot and prattling on about how lazy everyone else is compared to him.

Sure ways of getting rid of a grogoch include either inviting a clergyman into the home or offering him payment for his chores. This will offend him greatly, for the only thing a grogoch will accept as reward is a jug of buttermilk. Unlike a clergyman.

The grogoch's relatives, the laughremen, hail from the southern parts of Co. Armagh. Though similar in looks – both are infant-sized, sport a thick, reddish pelt and have the visage of an old man with a broad, flat nose – grogochs are generally well-meaning and occasionally useful while laughremen are actively malignant. Both are thought to be a species of leprechaun, and it is entirely possible that the word leprechaun came from laughremen, though this issue is hotly debated amongst folklorists. Laughremen are reputed to be ferocious guardians of the treasure of the old kings of Ulster situated at Navan Fort and will injure or kill

A lock of grogoch hair entangled with a chicken bone.

anyone who comes near it by pelting them with rocks[40].

Whilst on a research trip to Navan Fort, myself and a colleague were attacked by several laughremen. We managed to escape, with hurt pride the only injury sustained.

NOTES
Category: Solitary faery
Lifespan: Unknown
Habitat: Caves, human farms
Location: Counties Donegal, Antrim and South Armagh
Powers: Great strength. Hard worker.
See also: Leprechaun

39 In parts of counties Antrim and Donegal, a mother might tell her untidy son that he looks like an 'aul' grogoch'.
40 Being a native of South Armagh myself, I can testify that hairy, rock-throwing men were par for the course there, especially in the 1970s.

Leanan Sídhe

'FAERY MISTRESS'

Variations: leanhaun shee, lianhan shee, linane shie

I have never fallen prey to a leanan sídhe – otherwise my time on this earth would have been a good deal less than I've had the good fortune to experience. But I did know a young man – a close friend – who fell under the pishogue of one and paid the ultimate price.

My friend, whose name I shall give as Adam, was a final-year student at a well-known school of music in the city of Dublin. A natural adept at a wide range of instruments, including piano, violin, flute and cello, he also possessed a singing voice like that of a lovesick cherub. We shared a modest living space in the city with several other students of the arts.

One Friday afternoon, I had arranged to meet Adam at one of our regular watering-holes, but he failed to turn up at the appointed time. This was a peccadillo most unlike him, for Adam was usually pathologically early for appointments. I sat and waited alone for a few hours, sipping a single pint of stout in an effort to stretch out my meagre student purse.

When he did finally arrive, he was not alone. His habitually tidy hair was as unkempt as a hawthorn bush on a lonely mountain and his shirt buttons were tied in the wrong holes. He was giddy and breathless, giggling an apology like an infant caught pilfering sugar lumps from the pantry.

His companion, whom he did not deign to introduce, was a pasty-faced girl in dark, archaic attire with sleek black hair, high cheekbones, bloodless yet full lips and a gaze as cold as a white marble headstone. She regarded me icily as Adam blethered on about some composition he had penned just that afternoon, a piece so complex and difficult, he said, that it made Liszt's 'La Campanella' [41] seem like a novice pianist mangling the major scales.

He then dashed over to the vacant upright piano in the corner of the public house, his female associate gliding soundlessly after him, and began to play his piece. After just a few bars, the pub fell silent, every ear focused upon Adam's playing. Even the jaded barman ceased polishing glasses and marvelled at the incongruous sounds emanating from the rickety old piano, hitherto used only to bash out music hall songs and the occasional shanty.

When Adam finished, there was no applause, just a stunned silence. The crowd seemed unsure of what they had just witnessed – myself included, for I was frozen in place. Adam got off his stool and quickly exited, followed by the pale girl. As she left, she looked over her shoulder at me, smiling a smile that chilled my blood; a smile with no mirth attached, just malignance. It was then I realised what she was.

I dashed out onto the street to warn my friend, but he was nowhere to be seen. I never saw Adam again. He never returned to our digs, and failed to show up for any more classes or final exams. A mutual friend informed me not long after that he had been found dead, alone, in a foetid old garret, slumped over a new composition, looking like a man thrice his age.

A fragment of Adam's final composition.

NOTES

Category: Solitary faery

Lifespan: Unknown

Habitat: Anywhere that artists, poets and musicians congregate

Location: All over Ireland. In the west, the leanan sídhe is said to be relatively harmless.

Powers: WB Yeats said, 'The Leanhaun Shee seeks the love of mortals. If they refuse, she must be their slave; if they consent, they are hers, and can only escape by finding another to take their place. The fairy lives on their life, and they waste away. Death is no escape from her. She is the Gaelic muse, for she gives inspiration to those she persecutes.' [42]

See also: Gancanagh

41 'La Campanella' by Franz Liszt (1811–86) is famous as one of the most difficult pieces ever written for piano.
42 *Fairy and Folk Tales of the Irish Peasantry* (1888) by W.B. Yeats.

LEPRECHAUN

'LITTLE BODY'

Variations: clurichaun, leath chorpáin, lepreehawn, leprehaun, logheryman, lubrican, luricawne, lurigadawne

It may surprise the novice folklorist that there was no mention of the leprechaun before the medieval tale, 'Echtra Fergus mac Léti' (The Adventures of Fergus, Son of Leti). This describes the King of Ulster's encounter with three 'lúchorpáin', who grant him wishes in exchange for their release.

So whence they came? Legend has it that Danish Vikings put leprechauns in charge of their plundered gold, and Yeats says their vast wealth comes from 'treasure-crocks, buried of old in war-time'[43]. It is entirely possible that leprechauns are descendants of the fabled Scandinavian 'vættir'[44] and travelled to Ireland in Viking longboats.

The leprechaun is a solitary creature and thus cannot be categorised as one of the Aos Sí or the 'Good People'. Additionally, the leprechaun has a prankish nature and is not actively malignant towards folk, whereas the Aos Sí can, and will, harm or even kill humans.

I disagree with the common assertion that all leprechauns are shoe-makers or, in fact,

My leprechaun encounter occurred at none other than the legendary Hill of Tara, Co. Meath. I spotted this fellow in some undergrowth. He was around two feet tall and wore a dark red coat. I held his gaze – my father said always to do this with a faery, as you can gain temporary control over them. Tongue-tied, I said the first thing that came into my head: 'Isn't it a grand day?' He replied brashly, 'So the sun's out – should I be doing a cartwheel now?' I remembered then that leprechauns like a bit of banter and find 'yes' or 'no' answers boring, so I asked him, 'Why do faeries always answer a question with another question?' Quick as a rock falling, he replied, 'How should they answer?' and began to laugh. As soon as I blinked, he disappeared, his laughter ringing in my ears.

'the maker of one shoe'. This is likely based on a false etymology for the word leprechaun – from the Irish words 'leath' (half) and 'brógan' (shoes). What wealthy faery wants to spend time making or mending shoes?

They are certainly sneaky and protective of their wealth, as Thomas Crofton Croker recounts in his tale 'The Field of Boliauns'[45]. This is the story of a man who managed to catch a leprechaun and forced him to divulge the secret location of his treasure. The leprechaun reluctantly led him to a field of boliaun (ragweed) and pointed to a big ragweed shrub, saying, 'Dig under that boliaun, and you'll get the great crock all full of guineas.' Delighted, the man tied a red garter around the plant and ran home to fetch a spade. When he returned, he was dismayed to find every bit of ragweed in the field sporting the same red garter.

Speaking of the colour red, leprechauns are very fond of this hue and tend to wear red clothing, as well as a variety of hats. They range in size from around six inches to three feet tall.

Map of Tara from my *Handbook For Travellers in Ireland*, with the spot where I saw the leprechaun marked.

NOTES

Category: Solitary faery

Lifespan: Unknown

Habitat: Rural areas away from the general population; underground caves with doors disguised as rabbit holes; hollow tree trunks, especially hawthorns

Location: All over Ireland

Powers: Can disappear if you take your eyes off him; able to grant wishes

43 *Fairy and Folk Tales of the Irish Peasantry* (1888) by WB Yeats.
44 The faerie folk of the Norse peoples are known by this name.
45 *Fairy Legends and Traditions of the South of Ireland* (1825) by Thomas Crofton Croker.

MARBH BHEO

'LIVING DEAD'

Variations: *deamhan fola, dearg due, dearg dur, derrick-dally, murbhheo, vampire*

The word 'vampire' did not come into common usage in western Europe until the eighteenth century. It was virtually unheard of in Ireland until the publication of a story called 'Carmilla' by Irish author Joseph Sheridan le Fanu in 1872.[46] Ireland does have its equivalent of course – the marbh bheo. There are different kinds of marbh bheo – revenants who return corporeally from the grave for one reason or another – but here we are concerned only with the ones who drink blood to sustain their vile vigour.

Abhartach[47] was the tyrannical ruler of a small kingdom in Co. Derry in the sixth century. A practitioner of the black arts, he rose twice from his grave and terrorised his subjects, demanding their blood. He was finally put to rest, it's said, by Fionn mac

I spotted this marbh bheo returning from a night's imbibement to his grave in Roscrea, Co. Tipperary. Note the red eyes, indicating that he is engorged with his victims' blood. Luckily for me, he'd had his fill and the sun was about to rise.

Cumhaill himself. Even today, locals fear to tread the land near the lonely hawthorn tree where 'The Thrice-Buried Man' lies, head downwards, in his grave.[48]

Carrickaphouka Castle in Co. Cork was once the abode of Cormac Tadhg McCarthy, a sheriff appointed by the English to oversee the defeated but troublesome rebel Irish lords after the battle of Kinsale in 1601. One of those lords was a man named Fitzgerald. McCarthy invited him to dine at his castle on the pretence of brokering a peace agreement. Fitgerald's food was poisoned and McCarthy had his body drained of blood and cooked. He ate Fitzgerald's flesh and washed it down with flagons of his blood. It's said that after he died, McCarthy was resurrected by dark forces and continued to terrorise the area as a blood-drinking ghoul. Although today the castle lies in ruins, wails and tortured screams can be heard at night and at times the gate is seen splattered with fresh blood.

Throughout the country, tales of blood-suckers abound. In some places they are known as the 'dearg due' (red blood drinker), and in others 'deamhan fola' (blood demon), but they are all marbh bheo. Irishman Bram Stoker may have been inspired by these stories to write his own tale of an aristocratic blood-drinker in the recently published *Dracula*.[49]

During the Irish Great Hunger, there were those who drank blood out of sheer necessity. Desperate, starving people – literally the living dead – would make their way to a field under cover of darkness, open a vein in a cow's neck and drain a pint or so of blood into a jar. They sealed the wound with a wooden clip called a 'twitch'. The blood would be mixed with meal, herbs, turnip, wild mushrooms, milk, nettles or even grass to make a black pudding of sorts (euphemistically called a 'relish cake').

The true blood-drinkers were not these poor wretches, but the ones who owned the cattle and the fields in which they stood. For that land belonged to the hated landlords, who continually raised their tenants' rents, burned them out of their homes and bled them dry more mercilessly than any rapacious marbh bheo.

NOTES

Category: Revenant

Lifespan: Possibly immortal

Habitat: Ruined castles, crypts, graveyards near a ready supply of fresh blood.

Location: All over Ireland

Powers: Aside from the ability to return from the dead, they have enhanced strength, especially after feeding, and excellent night-vision.

See also: Fear gorta

46 The first vampire story published in English was *The Vampyre* (1819) by John William Polidori.
47 The tale of Abhartach first appeared in Patrick Weston Joyce's *The Origin and History of Irish Names of Places* (1870).
48 An attempt to clear the land in 1997 resulted in several accidents and an injury to a workman.
49 *Dracula* was first published on 16 May 1897, and was an absolute sensation.

MERROW

'SEA-MAIDEN'

Variations: maighdean-mhara, moruach, moruadh, muir-gheilt, murúch,
samguba, samhghubna, suire

The Irish version of the mermaid is the merrow. The word refers specifically to the female of the species, though the male is also often called this. Merrows are generally seen as having the top half of a human and the lower half of a fish, though there are many accounts of them looking entirely human except with flatter feet and webbed fingers. I can only surmise that some kind of magical metamorphosis occurs when a merrow comes ashore, or perhaps they shed their fishtails the way a reptile sloughs off its skin.

Merrows are exceptionally beautiful, with translucent skin that glows iridescently like sunlight on rippling water, hair that flows like a waterfall and large eyes as dark as the depths of the ocean. Thomas Crofton Croker must have been hungry when he wrote a description of a merrow thus: 'a beautiful young creature combing her hair, which was of a sea-green colour; and now the salt water shining on it, appeared, in the morning light, like melted butter upon cabbage.'[50]

I chanced upon this winsome merrow sunning herself at Murder Hole Beach, Co. Donegal. Note the little cap she wears, known as a 'cohuleen druith', which she must abandon in order to come ashore. Any human who finds this cap has power over the merrow, for she cannot return to the sea without it. Stories about it being made of feathers are nonsense – it is likely made from seal skin.

Male merrows are exceedingly ugly, with scaly green skin, seaweed-like hair, short, flipper-like arms, piggy eyes and noses and sharp green teeth. They are, unsurprisingly, rarely seen. Thomas Keightley[51] describes a fisherman's meeting with a merrow called Coomara (meaning sea-dog), who had a fish-tail as well as legs, a cumbersome and unlikely combination despite this sixteenth-century illustration from Conrad Gesner's *Historiae Animalium*.

The merrow species is said to originate from 'Tír fo Thoinn' (the Land Beneath the Waves), a vast underwater realm to the west of Ireland.

They may hail from the mythical island of Hy Brasil, recorded until recently on many maps.[52] Merrows are amphibious and can live a long time on land. They do, however, have an unnatural affinity for water and will spend as much time on land near it.

If a human man manages to steal the merrow's cohuleen druith and hides it well, he can persuade the merrow to marry and even have children with him. Perhaps not so difficult, when you consider what the males of the species look like. The offspring of such a union usually have scaly skin and webbed fingers. Though the merrow makes a good wife, she is often sullen and cold towards her human husband and children. Once she finds the cap, as she inevitably will, she'll think nothing of abandoning her life on land and returning to the sea.

Top right: A sketch of a merrow's hand. Above right: Merrows have a third eyelid[53] to protect their eyes, allowing them to see underwater.

NOTES

Category: Trooping faery

Lifespan: Thought to be many hundreds of years

Habitat: The sea, areas around coast, coastal caves. Sometimes spotted in rivers, though salt-water is their natural habitat.

Location: In the seas all round Ireland

Powers: Excellent swimmers. In some places, it is bad luck to see a merrow, as it can herald the coming of a bad storm. Merrow music has been heard from the depths of the ocean.

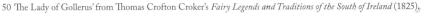

50 'The Lady of Gollerus' from Thomas Crofton Croker's *Fairy Legends and Traditions of the South of Ireland* (1825).
51 'The Soul Cages' by Thomas Keightley from Thomas Crofton Croker's *Fairy Legends and Traditions of the South of Ireland* (1825).
52 According to folklore, an island named Hy Brasil is visible from the west coast of Ireland for only one day every seven years, remaining obscured by fog the rest of the time. It was recorded on maritime maps for centuries, appearing on a British Admiralty Chart for the final time in 1873.
53 Many fish, amphibians, reptiles, birds and mammals have a nictitating membrane to protect the eye, first discovered by English biologist Richard Owen in 1866.

OILLIPHÉIST

'GREAT WORM'

Variations: horse eel, long-neck, payshta, péist, peiste, wurrum

Saint Patrick's driving the snakes out of Ireland[54] notwithstanding, stories of Irish heroes battling serpentine creatures go back to ancient times. One of them, the Táin Bó Fráech (Cattle Raid of Fráech), tells of a gallant warrior sent by Queen Medb to fetch some rowan berries from a tree guarded by an oilliphéist or 'great worm' – effectively an amphibious Irish dragon.

There have been relatively recent sightings of ollphéisteanna[55], however. An American newspaper reported a 100-foot-long creature off the west coast of Ireland that it called the Gorramooloch[56], which could 'rush through the water at the speed of an express train'. The same report mentions another beast it labels the Bo-dree-more, so large and powerful that it 'chases whales for sport'.

A sketch of an oilliphéist I observed one day whilst fishing on the shore of Muckross Lake in Co. Kerry. It had wings, but these appeared to be vestigial, like the forelimbs of the recently discovered Tyrannosaurus rex in the Americas[57]. It was around fifty feet long. The hide was smooth and green like that of a frog and its belly a lighter colour than the rest of its body.

Ireland's deep loughs are also home to freshwater oillphéisteanna. One legend has it that Ireland's holiest lake, Lough Derg ('Red Lake') in Co. Donegal, got its name after one of Fionn mac Cumhaill's Fianna warriors named Conan threw a hairy, worm-like creature into it. The worm grew into an enormous monster called Caoránach and devoured nearly all the cattle in Ulster[58]. Conan slew the creature, dyeing the rocks red with its blood.

Many of the boggy lakes in the Connemara region of Co. Galway contain 'horse-eels', which Thomas Crofton Croker describes as 'like a great big conger eel, seven yards long, and as thick as a bull in the body, with a mane upon his neck like a horse'.[59] One such beast was so big that it got wedged under a bridge near the castle at Ballynahinch, Connemara, in the summer of 1888. A thunderstorm flushed it away after two days. The bridge is about twelve feet high.

THE DAYS' DOINGS.

208

STARTLING APPEARANCE OF A MONSTER SEA-SERPENT OFF KILKEE ON THE IRISH COAST.—(FROM A SKETCH BY

A cutting from *The Days' Doings*, showing 'the startling appearance of a sea-serpent off Kilkee on the Irish coast'.

NOTES

Category: Rare water beast

Lifespan: Unknown. Perhaps centuries, though likely mortal

Habitat: The sea, loughs, lakes, deep pools

Location: Most sightings have occurred in the west of Ireland.

Powers: Powerful swimmers

54 There are no native species of snake in Ireland and no sign of any in its fossil record. These stories are likely metaphors for Saint Patrick's struggle with various pre-Christian potentates, pagan druids and serpent cults that Patrick and his minions all but eradicated from the land, hence 'driving the snakes out of Ireland'.
55 'Oillphéisteanna' is evidently the plural form of 'oillphéist'.
56 *The Herald Democrat*, 16 June 1922 edition published in Leadville, Colorado. 'Ireland Has Found Its Own Sea-serpent.'
57 The first T-rex skeleton was discovered in 1902 by the famous fossil hunter Barnum Brown in Hell Creek, Montana, USA.
58 This story is very similar to that of *The Lampton Worm*, a legend from the Northumberland region of England.
59 *Fairy Legends and Traditions of the South of Ireland* (1825) by Thomas Crofton Croker.

POOKA

'NATURE SPIRIT'

Variations: phooca, phooka, phouka, púca, puca, puck, pwca

According to some, Brian Ború was the only man ever to ride a pooka, using a special bridle strung with three hairs from the pooka's tail. What nonsense! For I, like many others, have gone on a 'wild ride' on the back of a pooka – and thankfully lived to tell the tale. I was very young and foolish. Had I the knowledge then that I have now, I would not have dared approach, never mind mount, this mischievous faerie creature.

One balmy evening in April, I had disembarked my train at the tiny station of Grange Con, Co. Wicklow,[60] when I heard a voice call out, 'Do ye want a ride?' I was taken aback, as there was no one but me on the platform. Thinking it was my imagination, I said nothing and quickly left the station, bound for my aunt's house in the village.

The voice came again: 'I said, do ye want a ride?' The head and neck of a black colt appeared from behind a tree and I assumed the voice belonged to the colt's rider, still obscured by the tree trunk. But the muscular young horse walked out to reveal no passenger and stood boldly before me. Its golden, gleaming eyes transfixed me.

'Did you … did you just speak?' I said stupidly, but the colt remained silent. Thinking he had strayed from a local stable, I approached and he allowed me to stroke his nose. I was a half-decent rider in my youth, so I mounted the horse, thinking I could return him to his proper owner and be hero for a day. What a mistake that was.

As soon as I was upon the colt's back, he bolted forward with a terrifying velocity that should have unseated me. Miraculously I remained upright, gripping the flowing black mane as the colt leaped over the nearby River Greese and dove into some gorse bushes. The thorns tore at my clothes and skin. I only narrowly avoided having an eye put out more than once, as tree branches whipped dangerously past my head.

This hellish gallop took me o'er bogs and shucks[61], through briars and nettles, into rivers and ditches until finally, the beast deposited me roughly in a stony field, winding me as I hit the ground. I thought I heard demented laughter emanating form the colt's mouth as it dashed away into nearby undergrowth, but that may have been just the wind.

I was bruised, scratched and cut, my clothing in disarray, gorse spikes emanating from my coat. And I'd lost my favourite cap. But at least I was alive. I limped the many miles back to Grange Con village, where my aunt, with whom I was meant to be staying, greeted me with shock and surprise. 'You were supposed to be here yesterday!' she cried. Indeed, I could feel the light of the dawning sun upon my cheek as I stepped into her house. My 'wild ride' had lasted all night.

Some of the pooka's mane-hairs.

NOTES

Category: Solitary faery

Lifespan: Unknown

Habitat: Thick woodlands

Location: All over Ireland, mostly rural and wooded areas; hills and mountains

Powers: Can shape-shift into many different forms, but mostly that of a sleek black horse with luminescent golden eyes. Also seen as a goblin, bull, goat, wolf, fox, eagle, bat, dog, cat, hare, rabbit and occasionally a human, but with some animal features such as hooves or a tail. Can speak with a human voice. Can befoul crops and fruits, though this may be something told to children to prevent them from eating overripe blackberries.

See also: Aughisky

60 Grange Con was the smallest station on the Great Southern & Western Railway's branch line from Sallins to Tullow. It opened in 1885 and closed in 1947.

61 A shuck or sheugh is a drainage ditch that runs along the bottom of a field, perhaps Ulster-Scots in origin and used all over the northern parts of the country. Not to be confused with Black Shuck, a demon dog that roams the fens of East Anglia, England. Also slang for the space between one's buttocks.

SHEERIE

Variations: corpse candle, fetch candle, fetch light, ignis fatuus

In Greenland not long ago, a most curious and ugly fish washed up on the shore, almost perfectly spherical with a gigantic mouth filled with razor-sharp fangs. Most unusual of all was the proboscis of flesh that protruded from its head, a light of sorts that performed the function of luring other fish towards it … and straight into its gaping maw.[62]

My brother Fintan and I were walking home one evening after cutting turf on Turf Mountain, Co. Louth, when a sheerie attempted to lure us into a bog-hole.

The faerie equivalent of this fish is the sheerie, but instead of the dark Arctic depths, the sheerie's hunting grounds are the boglands of Ireland. If you happen to be traversing a bog at twilight – who knows your reason as to why – be watchful for hovering balls of light that bob and weave like lanterns carried by fellow travellers. Do not follow these lights, for not only will you never get near them, but they will lead you off the path to a lonely, watery grave.

at all, but spirit-guides of some kind. Like the fetch, they are not necessarily malevolent. Different coloured lights may indicate who is going to die.

There's a charming story about a rogue called Stingy Jack[63] who makes a deal with the Devil, offering up his soul in exchange for payment of his sizeable pub tab. Of course, Jack wriggles out of the deal, but the Devil won't allow him to enter Hell when he dies.

Large red light: Adult male

Small blue light: Child

Pale blue light: Toddler or infant

Large white light: Adult woman

Two orbs of varying size side by side: A woman and her unborn child

In some places, these luminescent balls of light are thought to be the souls of unbaptised children, but I would hasten to disagree. What innocent babe would want to harm a living human? In other places, they are similar to the banshee – an omen of imminent death. They often trace the path a funeral procession will soon be travelling, all the way to the graveyard. These are known as 'fetch candles' and I would argue that they are not sheerie

Old Nick does give Jack an ember from his infernal fires to light his way through the twilight world to which Jack's soul is condemned. Jack places it in a carved turnip to serve as a lantern. A nice story, but if you think that you're following Stingy Jack's lantern some night when you're traversing a bog, you'd do well to remember the ugly fish that washed up in Greenland and festinate in the opposite direction.

NOTES

Category: Solitary faery

Lifespan: Unknown

Habitat: Inland bodies of water, bogs, marshes, wetlands, graveyards

Location: All over Ireland

Powers: Flight, bio-luminescence

See also: Banshee, The Devil, Fetch

62 The anglerfish came to attention when a female specimen washed ashore in Greenland in 1833. It was later dubbed the 'footballfish' or 'man-gobbler' by Norwegian-Danish zoology professor Johannes Christopher Hagemann Reinhardt. To date, 170 species of anglerfish are known to science.

63 The Romance of Jack O'Lantern is a poem written by Hercules Ellis in 1851.

SKEAGH SHEE

'TREE FAERY'

Variations: lunatishee, oak shee, sheoque

'Whitethorn (hawthorn) was considered a sacred tree. When it grows alone near the banks of a stream, or on forts, it is considered to be the haunt and peculiar abode of the fairies, and as such is not to be disturbed without risk, sooner or later, of personal danger to the person so offending.'[64]

The faeries who are guardians of these so-called faerie trees are named skeagh shee after the Irish word 'sceach', meaning thorn-bush, but they are known to dwell in other trees as well.

Faerie trees are easily identifiable. They often stand alone in fields or by the side of the road and sometimes have large stones circling the base. They are most often found in isolated areas of the countryside, sometimes on or near ringforts, under which are faerie dwellings. Early Irish sources talk of the 'bile rátha' (sacred tree of the fort), which acted

I spotted this skeagh shee whilst sketching a faerie tree in a field near Carrick-on-Shannon, Co. Leitrim. It watched me for some time, presumably in case I meant the tree harm. When it realised I didn't, it seemed to just blend in with the trunk, though I could still feel it watching me.

as assembly points for faerie armies. They may also be markers on a faerie path.

Faerie trees have a somewhat unusual appearance – often more gnarled than normal, with elongated trunks or exposed roots. They may have more thorns than typical, or no thorns at all, and may never blossom. They might continue to grow even after being uprooted, though to uproot a faerie tree is very ill-advised. It's common for farmers to work around these trees, even when when it causes them great inconvenience.

The word 'sceach' is also used to describe a prickly, quarrelsome person and skeagh shee are certainly that. Skeagh shee can, and do, inflict ill luck, madness, disease, paralysis, blindness, baldness, maiming, poverty and death upon anyone who molests or cuts down a tree under their protection – and often on that person's family too. The skeagh shee have a strong bond with their trees and have been heard wailing and crying when one is damaged or cut down.

By the craggy hillside,
Through the mosses bare,
They have planted thorn trees
For my pleasure, here and there.
Is any man so daring
As dig them up in spite,
He shall find their sharpest thorns
In his bed at night.[65]

Although it was early summer, this little leaf fell from the tree and landed right in my sketch book, just as I had finished drawing.

NOTES

Category: Solitary faery

Lifespan: Unknown

Habitat: Isolated trees, usually hawthorn but also associated with alder, ash, blackthorn, elder, hazel, holly, oak and rowan. Lunatishee (moon faeries) are the particular guardians of blackthorn and hawthorn trees.

Location: All over Ireland

Powers: Can cause great harm to anyone who damages or fells a faerie tree.

64 *Traces of the Elder Faiths in Ireland: A Folklore Sketch* (1903) by William Gregory Wood-Martin.
65 'The Fairies' (1850) by William Allingham.

SLUAGH NA MARBH

'HOST OF THE DEAD'

Variations: Host of the unforgiven dead, sleagh math, sluagh, sluagh sidhe, the wild hunt, underfolk

The sluagh na marbh ride forth from the west in 'the mouth of the night', seeking souls to steal. To this day, doors and windows on the west sides of houses are kept locked if there is a sick or dying person at home. The most dangerous time is at Samhain[66], the 'feile na marbh' (festival of the dead) at the end of October, when the veil between this earthly realm and the Otherworld is at its thinnest.

The sluagh appear as a whirlwind of flapping wings and undulating shadows, much like a murder of crows, themselves carrion birds associated with death. A closer look will reveal them to be humanoid in appearance though

I was attending the wake of a dear friend in Hawkswood, Co. Longford, when the house was set upon by the sluagh. We were pelted with projectiles and elf-bolts[67] for some time, until the sluagh eventually tired and flew away.

somewhat haggard with leathery wings, beak-like mouths and clawed hands and feet.

Should you see a sinister, dark mass heading towards you from the western skies, it would behoove you to get indoors as soon as humanly possible, and shut all the doors and windows. If there is no shelter nearby, wedge yourself in the crevice of a rock or use your belt or a length of rope to lash yourself to a strong tree. Avoid bridges and crossroads at all costs, as they are favoured hunting grounds of the sluagh.

It's said you should hurl your left shoe at the sluagh before you are snatched, but this is not sure to work. What is sure is you will be missing one shoe. Turning your coat inside out and saying the incantation 'My face from you, my back to you' may confuse the sluagh long enough to attempt an escape. Sacrificing another in your stead is the only sure way to save yourself, but it would be difficult to live with such a vile deed afterwards.

Being in the wrong place at the wrong time notwithstanding, it is possible to inadvertently call the sluagh to you, by two means. One is by mere utterance of the word 'sluagh'; the other is through the silent hopelessness in one's heart. The sluagh can home in on the crushing weight of sadness like a sparrow-hawk swooping down on a shrew. That's not to say that the sluagh won't pursue the light of spirit – they certainly will. It's just easier to peel away the soul of a despondent person than a happy one.

In pagan Ireland, it was believed the sluagh were rogue faeries running amok. After Christianity arrived, they were seen as the host of the unforgiven dead – those who died by suicide or the souls of unbaptised children, led by none other than the Devil himself, busying himself with the aggregation of more souls for his infernal kingdom.

The sluagh do sometimes return their victims after a time, though with battered bodies and addled wits. The victim will certainly never be the same again.

An elf-bolt I recovered from outside the wake house.

NOTES

Category: Undead revenants or rogue faeries.
Lifespan: Immortal.
Habitat: Skies to the west.
Location: All over Ireland.
Powers: The power of flight, though they may more accurately glide on a 'faerie wind'.
See also: The Devil

66 Samhain is the most important of the Celtic seasonal festivals, along with Imbolc, Bealtaine and Lughnasa. It marks the beginning of the Celtic new year, at the midpoint between the autumn equinox and the winter solstice.
67 Elf-bolts look awfully like Neolithic flint arrow heads.

STRAY SOD

Variations: faerie grass, faud shaughran, fód seachrán, fóidín mearaí, foidin mhara, foidin seacrain

There is a breed of faery that will make a traveller lose their way, no matter how familiar the surroundings. It can also cause a maddening urge to walk all night, through bogs and over hills, until the traveller finds himself, exhausted, twenty or thirty miles from his point of origin. Some folklorists say it is merely a clump of vegetation enchanted by the faeries, or a cursed patch of ground growing on the graves of unbaptised children, but I say they are talking through their hats. It is a faery creature, the stray sod.

Once, crossing a field in Gneeveguilla, Co. Kerry, I trod upon a stray sod. I immediately forgot which way I was going and walked around and around looking for a way out. I remembered then my mother telling me that if this should ever happen, to turn my coat inside out and put it back on. This I did, and instantly regained my way.

A second encounter occurred near my home in South Armagh, in a spot well known to me. This time, the coat-turning did not work, so I took off my shoes, put them on the wrong feet and spun around thrice. The way out became obvious to me then. Another time, I kept a close eye on a hare, which made its speedy way to the nearest exit.

This same disorientation can occur if one wanders into a faerie ring or fort, which are likely guarded by stray sods. Tales have been told of luckless individuals who have been magically transported to the faerie realm and come out again greatly aged, for time passes differently there. If indeed they come out at all.

Is there a real-world equivalent of the stray sod that occurs in nature? In Latin America there are tales of a tree that uproots itself and walks away if it doesn't like where it is.[68]

Some slow-moving animals have also been seen carrying sizeable wads of soil and grass on their backs.[69]

It is possible that the stray sod's propensity to lead travellers astray is some kind of defence mechanism. After all, if you were a diminutive faerie creature, minding your own business out in a field, would you desire to be trod upon by a clumsy human? Just as a hedgehog curls into a ball if a predator is nearby, the stray sod will disorientate the traveller until it can find a means of escape. Of course, the stray sod could simply be acting mischievously, as faeries are wont to do.

Many hundreds of people go missing in Ireland every year.[70] While most of them are thankfully found, many are not, and it is possible some have fallen victim to the stray sod. They may still be wandering the hills in a daze or may have ended up in the faerie realm, fate unknown.

NOTES

Category: Faery beast

Lifespan: Unknown

Habitat: Faerie fields and paths

Location: All over Ireland

Powers: Causes severe disorientation. Appears slightly greener than its neighbouring grass. May protect leprechaun gold. Could have magical properties if eaten, but best not to find out.

68 The Walking Palm (*Socrateaa exorrhiza*) can move up to 2–3 centimetres per day, the tree's stilt-like roots enabling it to 'walk' towards better-growing conditions, such as more sunlight or better soil. The Walking Palm is an important plant in traditional medicine, its bark being been used to treat fever, malaria and snake bites.

69 The Common snapping turtle (*Chelydra serpentina*) often gets covered in mud during hibernation. This mud sometime sprouts vegetation, making the turtle look like a walking garden when it wakes up.

70 Official Garda statistics state that 10,509 people were reported missing in 2022. Nearly 9,700 were reported missing in Northern Ireland in the same year, making quite a sizeable sum for the whole island.

TARBH-UISCE

'WATER-BULL'

Variations: Irish hippopotamus

Long nights of waiting for a tarbh-uisce to appear were rewarded when I spotted this magnificent specimen emerge from Lough Gur, Co. Limerick, near a field of cattle. Note the short ears, similar to those of a hippopotamus, as well as the clubbed feet. We watched each other a while and once he sensed I was no threat, he had his way with several of the cows. His bellowing reminded me of a crowing rooster, but much lower in pitch. He slipped back into the lough shortly before first light.

The tarbh-uisce is a faery beast not often glimpsed in Ireland, due to its nocturnal nature. Although he has the general appearance of a large black bull, he is fairly docile and surfaces from loughs at night to graze and mate with ordinary cattle.

The offspring of the tarbh-uisce are half-faerie. Known as 'split-ears', their ears are much shorter than those of conventional cattle. In places like the Scottish Inner Hebrides, calves born with malformed ears are often slaughtered to protect the herd from ill-fortune. In other places, however, the progeny of water-bulls are much valued and can fetch hefty sums at market.

Cows and bulls have always enjoyed a special place in Irish folklore, with the Táin Bó Cúailnge being just one famous example.[71] Indeed, Lady Wilde relates that the first cattle were introduced to Ireland by a mermaid named Berooch.[72]

She brought forth from the Atlantic three magnificent sacred cows, 'all beautiful to behold, with sleek skins, large soft eyes, and curved horns, white as ivory'. They were Bó Finn, the white cow, Bó Rua, the red cow, and Bó Dubh, the black cow, 'who were destined to fill the land with the most splendid cattle, so that the people should never know want while the world lasted'.

If you desired to capture or kill a tarbh-uisce, you would have your work cut out for you. He can be angled for using sheep as bait, though the tackle has yet to be made that would hold him. It's said that this elusive beast is vulnerable to silver, much like its water-dwelling cousin the dobhar-chú. A story tells of a Scottish farmer and his two sons who hunted a water-bull with a musket loaded with silver sixpences,[73] though personally I'd rather use my money on something quaffable than waste it slaying a relatively harmless tarbh-uisce.

NOTES

Category: Faery beast

Lifespan: Unknown

Habitat: Isolated pools, lakes, bogs, rivers; has also been spotted in saltwater offshore

Location: Mostly the west of Ireland

Powers: Amphibious; brutish strength

See also: Aughisky, Dobhar-chú

71 *The Táin Bó Cúailnge* (The Cattle Raid of Cooley) is an epic from the Ulster Cycle of Irish mythology, relating the war between Queen Medb of Connacht and her husband King Ailill of Ulster over the ultra-fertile brown bull of Cooley, Donn Cúailnge.
72 *Ancient Legends, Mystic Charms, and Superstitions of Ireland* (1888) by Lady Jane Francesca Wilde.
73 *A Description of the Western Islands of Scotland, Volume 2* (1819) by John MacCulloch.

WEREWOLF

'MAN-WOLF'

Variations: conriocht, faoladh, luchthonn, lycanthrope, wolf-man

Unlike their fully animal brethren, werewolves are still alive and well in Ireland. My startling encounter with this brute was at the Rock of Dunamase, Co. Laois, just as a full moon was on the rise one night – I had neglected to check my almanac for phases of the moon. Luckily, I was downwind of him, or I could have ended up as his supper. I heard the next day that several cattle were eviscerated in the area.

Wolves were once so populous in Ireland that it was nicknamed 'Wolf Land'. They were such a problem for English settlers that the insidious Oliver Cromwell offered 'for every bitch wolfe, six pounds; for every dogg wolfe, five pounds; for every cubb which prayeth for himself, forty shillings; for every suckling cubb, ten shillings.'[74] The last wild wolf was eventually slain in Co. Carlow in 1786, for allegedly devouring sheep.

The Fianna warriors of old – landless youths who dwelt in the wilderness – were known as 'luchthonn' (wolf-skins), because they wore the pelts of wolves they'd slaughtered. They so terrorised the local population with their feral appearance that they were thought to literally *be* wolves.

The *Annals of the Four Masters*[75] records that in the year 690, 'The wolf was heard speaking with human voice, which was horrific to all.' Norsemen spoke of a creature in Ireland that 'was caught in the forest as to which no one could say definitely whether it was a man or some other animal; for no one could get a word from it or be sure that it understood human speech. It had the human shape, however, in every detail, both as to hands and face and feet; but the entire body was covered with hair as the beasts are, and down the back it had a long coarse mane like that of a horse, which fell to both sides and trailed along the ground when the creature stooped in walking.'[76]

The *Cóir Anmann* (Fitness of Names)[77] tells of a warrior who 'used to go wolfing, i.e. into wolf-shapes, i.e. into shapes of wolves he used to go, and his offspring used to go after him and they used to kill the herds after the fashion of wolves, so that it is for that that he used to be called Laignech Fáelad, for he was the first of them who went into a wolf-shape'.

Not all Irish werewolves spent their time worrying sheep or terrorising their communities. The famous tale 'The Werewolves of Ossory', as told by that most mendacious of monks, Gerald of Wales,[78] recounts a priest's encounter with a benevolent werewolf and his sick wife, to whom the priest gives last rites. However, kindly werewolves are very much the exception, and these ferocious were-beasts should be avoided at all costs.

NOTES

Category: Cursed humans. Lycanthropy[79] is an affliction that runs in families.

Lifespan: Same as a human. Said to be vulnerable to silver bullets

Habitat: They favour rural areas away from people and near a food source.

Location: Mostly associated with the ancient kingdom of Osraigh (Ossory), now modern-day Co. Kilkenny and western Co. Laois, but can be found all over Ireland.

Powers: Shape-shifting, especially on a full moon. Great hunting prowess. Enhanced sight and olfactory abilities.

74 *Declaration touching Wolfes*, issued in 1652.

75 *The Annals of the Four Masters* is a chronicle of medieval Irish history, compiled between 1632 and 1636.

76 From the thirteenth-century Norse text, *Konungs Skuggsjá* (The King's Mirror), written for the education of prince Magnus Lagabøte, heir to King Hákon Hákonsson. In the form of a dialogue between a father and son, this section is from a chapter called 'The Natural Wonders of Ireland'. It is likely a retelling of 'The Werewolves of Ossory'.

77 The *Cóir Anmann* is a medieval Irish work that explains the significance and associations of many personal names from early Ireland.

78 Gerald of Wales aka Giraldus Cambrensis aka Gerald de Barri (1146–1223) was a Cambro-Norman priest who travelled to Ireland in 1185 with the future King John of England. Gerald wrote the *Topographia Hiberniae* (Topography of Ireland). To say it has a rather heavy prejudice against the Irish would be the pinnacle of understatement.

79 From the Greek *lykos*, 'wolf', and *anthropos*, 'man'.

ᗷPRONUNCIATION ᗷUIDE

The Irish language is complex and can be a challenge to the tongue for non-natives. What follows is a rough guide to the pronunciation of the names of most of the creatures, and types of creatures, found in this book. There are also regional and dialectical variations in pronunciation, so it is not intended to be definitive, merely approximate.

Alp-luachra   *Alp-loo-cra*
Amadán   *Amma-dan*
Aos sí   *Ees-she*
Aughisky   *Aw-giss-kee*
Banshee   *Ban-she*
Cailleach   *Callick*
Clurichaun   *Cloor-eh-hawn*
Dobhar-chú   *Dower-koo*
Dullahan   *Dull-a-han*
Fear dearg   *Far-jar-ig*
Fear gorta   *Far-gor-ta*
Fear liath   *Far-lee-ah*
Fetch   *Fetch*
Gancanagh   *Gan-canna*
Grogoch   *Grow-gock*
Leanan sídhe   *Lee-ann-she*
Leprechaun   *Lep-reh-hawn*
Marbh bheo   *Mar-vee-oh*
Merrow   *Mer-oh*
Oilliphéist   *Awl-lee-fest*
Pooka   *Poo-ka*
Sheerie   *Sheer-ee*
Sheoque   *She-oak*
Skeagh shee   *Ska-shee*
Sluagh na marbh   *Sloo-ah-nah-marv*
Tarbh-uisce   *Tarv-ish-keh*
Thivish   *Thiv-ish*

AFTERWORD

Shortly before this book was due to go to press, I ran into my uncle Kevin at the only place my relatives and I ever seem to meet these days: a family funeral. My elderly uncle Bob, grandson of Fantasius's youngest sister Betsy, had apparently suffered a brain aneurysm whilst laughing at a cat video on YouTube. At least he died happy.

Kevin made a beeline for me at the do after the funeral, just as I was stuffing an egg and onion sandwich into my face. (I love egg and onion sandwiches, but you wouldn't want to be around me about an hour after I had one.) I nearly dived under the table in case he wanted me to paint the outside of his new house or something, but it was too late – he'd seen me.

'I hear you're doing a book about the fairies,' he said.

'I am. From that box of stuff you gave me.'

'Well, I told you you'd like it. The only thing is, I can't let you use any of it. You certainly can't publish it.'

I almost choked on my sandwich. 'What?!? Why not?!?'

He burst into laughter. 'Jaysus, I'm only messing with you. You near turned the colour of that tablecloth! Here, I wanted to give you this. Bob, God rest him, gave it to me when he heard you were doing the book.'

From his jacket pocket he drew out a yellowing photo of my great-granduncle Fantasius, looking fit and healthy in his late seventies. I stared at the photo and Fantasius stared back at me through the decades. I'd spent so many hours with this man's words and pictures that I felt I knew him.

But now, to see those dark eyes gazing into my soul, I wasn't so sure I knew him at all. The photo seemed to raise more questions than it answered.

'You can keep that,' said Kevin, walking off, 'but if you do another book, I want twenty percent.'

– John Farrelly, Newry, Co. Down.

Fantasius F. Farrelly, 1947